Rhys Hughes

CLOUD FARMING IN WALES

Rhys Hughes was born in Wales but has lived in many different countries. He graduated as an engineer and currently works as a tutor of mathematics. He began writing fiction at an early age and his first book, *Worming the Harpy,* was published in 1995. Since that time he has published more than thirty other books. His short stories have been translated into ten languages. He is nearing the end of an ambitious project to complete a cycle of exactly one thousand linked tales. His most recent book is the collection *The Seashell Contract* and he is hard at work on an experimental novel called *Comfy Rascals*. Fantasy, humour, satire, science fiction, adventure, irony, paradoxes and philosophy are combined in his work to create a distinctive style.

RHYS HUGHES

CLOUD FARMING IN WALES

THIS IS A SNUGGLY BOOK

ISBN: 978-1-943813-36-0

CLOUD FARMING IN WALES

On the slope of the hill stands a curious figure. It is a man in a smock and floppy hat. His beard is very long and he holds a crook. The crook makes no effort to escape because it's not an apprehended criminal but a twisted staff. The staff makes no attempt to go on strike because it is not the staff of an exploitative firm but a length of wood. The man gazes directly out of the page and begins to speak as follows:

"Cloud Farming is the life for me, and since I started cloud farming I have never looked back, my neck is too stiff. I get up early and go late to bed because clouds require little sleep."

Behind him, clouds drift over the slope, very low to the ground, most of them white but a few black and ominous. Some are small and playful, foolish clouds, lamb cumulus, adorable.

The man sighs and adds, "Once a year I dip my clouds. It's important for a cloud farmer to do this. Today is the day I must dip my entire flock, one by one, and that's what is going to happen next. Sheep are dipped in liquid, but clouds are already made of liquid, so that's not the best thing to dip them in. It simply wouldn't work."

Shifting his crook to his other hand and adjusting the brim of his hat, he manages a thin smile. "Indeed no. Clouds must be dipped in the minds of men and women, in the conscious regard of human beings. One by one, numbered so that all are accounted for, with the cloudlets following their mothers. That's how we dip our clouds."

His meaning is clear. He wants you, dear reader, to prepare yourself, for you are the dip. This is how cloud farming is done in these parts. The mind of a stranger is always welcome here. There won't be splashing, not much anyway, so don't worry about that.

As this figure turns to whistle for his clouds, you may perceive that he has a large key protruding from his back.

Wales is a small country with a small population. The sheep outnumber the people; the clouds outnumber the sheep. Many long ages ago, or so it is said, the land was crammed with human beings. The population density was so high that men and women were packed together side by side and there was no room to sit down. The sheer weight of inhabitants caused the entire country to sink below sea level.

The waves surged over everything and people had to hold their breath but those that couldn't hold it long enough drowned and their dead bodies floated away. The weight on the landmass was lessened. Eventually, there wasn't enough combined mass to keep the country down and it sprang up again, and only those inhabitants with bigger lungs survived. This is why Wales seems to be a nation of singers.

The survivors use those bigger lungs to sing and also to shout to each other across distances. Farmers on remote farms don't need telephones in order to communicate. They simply open a window and bellow out into the rain and somebody far away will hear them, even if it's not the person the message is intended for. The message might be, "Sheep farming's no good, let's try cloud farming instead!"

[10]

The clouds that drift perpetually in the sky above Wales are the ghosts of the drowned citizens from ancient times. The rains that fall forever are the tears of the ghosts. The ghosts are upset at not being alive; or perhaps they want to flood the country to remind the descendants of the survivors what it was like when Wales auditioned to be Atlantis but didn't make the grade. This, at any rate, is one theory . . .

The figure on the hill with the hat and the crook is someone I have known for quite a while. He has at least one saying for every occasion; and even more sayings for moments that aren't occasions at all. "Every death has a flavour and the taste of their demise is the last sensation any human being can enjoy," is one of his favourites.

I asked him to explain this insight in more detail. He replied that when one is clubbed to death by an apeman the flavour's salty; if fatally mauled by an affronted puma it is sour; when tumbling off a jagged precipice it is bitter; if bashed on the noggin by a meteorite then sweetness is dominant. This last word sticks in my mind. Clouds are the dominant life-form in the land. Welsh citizens are submissive.

Combinations of dooms and tastes are not only possible but desirable if one likes variety. To be pierced by an arrow and then beheaded with an axe is more like a proper meal than just experiencing one of those attacks. He informs me that drowning is the most mouth-watering of deaths but he scowls when I chuckle. He's serious.

He wasn't always a cloud farmer. In fact he once had aspirations to be a writer, but embarrassment forced him to seek alternative employment. I will say more about this soon enough. In Wales people can drown where they stand, without needing to plunge into rivers or the sea. The rain is so plentiful that it often completely fills their mouths, their throats, those big lungs of theirs. Wetly they expire. Nowhere else in the wide world will a person drown walking along a street.

Sure, it's an exaggeration to say that it never stops raining in Wales, that it has been raining without pause for millions of years. That is merely the way it *feels* rather than the way it is. The truth is that whole minutes, even full hours, might pass in which the sky is dry. These occasions are rare. It is far more likely that you will sight a phoenix in flight than not get wet in Wales. But they happen. Yes they do.

> *"What are you writing about, Bruce?"*
>
> *"Wales, Diana."*
>
> *The lower lip shot forward. Her painted cheeks swivelled through an angle of ninety degrees.*
>
> *"Whales!" she said. "Blue whales! . . . Sperrrm whales! . . . The White Whale!"*
>
> *"No . . . no, Diana! Wales! Welsh Wales! The country to the west of England."*
>
> *"Oh! Wales. I do know Wales. Little grey houses . . . covered in roses . . . in the rain. . . ."*
>
> (Bruce Chatwin in conversation with Diana Vreeland)

Wales is famous, if famous is quite the right word, for sheep and clouds, and yet the obvious connection between them is rarely remarked upon. I think many people haven't even noticed.

Clouds are sky sheep; there is no other way of stating this truth. Sheep lacking legs and heads. They aren't held back by any of the disadvantages that come with missing anatomy, no sir! Clouds are eminently successful entities that have made a good home here.

Well, that's one way of looking at it, but there is another way, namely that sheep are ground clouds. I was walking in Wales, tramping across a field far from any town, when it began to rain. The trees were all bare of leaves; there was nowhere to take shelter.

Then it occurred to me that I could shelter under a sheep. Why not? A sheep is waterproof, and unlike an umbrella does not generally blow inside out in the gales that frequently accompany rain in Wales. The field I was in was full of sheep. So that is what I did.

No sooner had I crawled under a suitable sheep than the rain stopped. The sun shone brightly in a blue sky. But it started raining where I was, a terrific downpour that came from the body of the sheep itself. Drenched, I quickly rolled back out into the open field.

The blue sky vanished as I did so. It was raining again, heavily, and a fistful of slimy raindrops punched me in the face. I saw that the sheep had stopped raining, that it was dry under there, so I crawled under the animal a second time. Then the blue sky returned.

I tried other sheep, every sheep in that field, but it made no difference. When I was in the open, the sky rained but the sheep didn't. When I was under a sheep, the sky took a rest and the sheep did the work. They were colluding to ensure that I became saturated.

Because a man isn't a man in Wales, and a woman isn't a woman, if that man and that woman aren't saturated; and this is a natural law that is futile to oppose. I know what you are thinking. Did the sheep get smaller the more they rained? Yes, I reply, they did.

Sheep that have rained heavily for weeks on end shrink so much that they end up being far too small to shelter under. These are called lambs. It is a myth that lambs are baby sheep. On the contrary, lambs are old sheep that have rained every drop of their moisture.

If a lamb continues to rain, and they always do, they eventually shrink to the point of non-existence. That is why the sheep you see in a field one year probably won't be the same sheep you see next year. They've rained themselves away, for they are ground clouds.

This is a work in progress right now.

It will no longer be a work in progress by the time it reaches you and you read these words. Then it will have become a finished work, at least to all intents and purposes, although I guess I can always alter it for future republication, so maybe it'll always be a work in progress on some level, and perhaps we too, human beings, are works in progress as we progress through life the way we write a book.

But I simply can't regard it as a finished work.

I do have the option of deleting this section when the work is finished, but I don't want to do that. However, to prove that I could actually do this easily, I will delete the following line.

. .. .

It wasn't an especially good line, by the way, which is why I found it so easy to sacrifice in that manner. Indeed it was intended as a sacrifice from the very beginning, to make a point.

What it actually said was, "This is a sacrificial line."

Not all deletions are authentic.

Types of WIPS

A work in progress is known as a WIP.

If it's not going anywhere or saying anything sensible, but wallowing in its own falsity, then it is a Bull-WIP.

If it can go several places, as yet undecided, and say several things, as yet undetermined, it is a Cat o'Nine Tales.

If it lacks depth, it is a Paddle.

If it needs to be radically cut and edited then it is a Reading Crop.

If it flutters alluringly, winks seductively or blinks nervously around the ego of its author, it's a lash, an I-Lash.

If the author seems Able, then it's a Cane.

This very text is a WIP, I'm unsure of what kind.

But, as I've already pointed out, it is only temporarily a WIP, while I am writing it, and by the time you read these words, namely the words declaring this text to be a WIP, assuming that you do read them, it will no longer be a WIP but a finished product.

A work not in progress.

That will sting less, a lot less, one hopes. . . .

When a character in this story by the name of Wilson learned that he was a writer, he became anxious, because the device of the fictional writer is an unappealing one. I am not sure why this should be the case, but it is. When I start to read a novel or short story and discover that the narrator or one of the important protagonists is a writer, I grow despondent. Most of the time I rapidly lose interest in the work. It seems to me at this point that the author needs to get out more, as if writing is the only thing he or she knows about, and that is why they have made that particular character a writer too. It is bad practice, a narrow, shallow and confined stratagem that is little better than a cheap trick. It is a narcissistic to an extent, yes, but the aspect that most oppresses me about this recourse is that it is very indolent. It smacks of a lack of imagination.

My luggage is also narrow, shallow and confined, and again I am not sure why this should be the case, but it is my case, a battered but elegant vulcanite container in which I convey an oboe between the teeming cities of the world. This is something we will discuss later. In the meantime, let us return to Wilson and his anxiety. He found out that he was supposed to be a writer in this story and he decided to take immediate evasive action. He reminded himself that he was a free man and under no obligation at all to write anything. So he began to look for other ways of defining himself to the public, to you out there reading this right now. He drew attention to the other activities that constituted a typical Wilson day, in the hope that a new definition of his persona would emerge. He stressed his hobbies over his profession. So what were those hobbies?

He liked to read books, but who can convincingly answer that they are a reader when asked what they do for a living, apart from reviewers and a few specialists employed by publishing companies? He enjoyed twiddling his thumbs, but twiddler is another unpersuasive career. His bicycle was a possession he had much respect for, but physically he looked nothing like the kind of cyclist who wins competitions and makes money as a result. A fondness for astronomy was part of his nature and he thought it would be nice to build a radio telescope in his garden, but the project remained only a daydream. His garden was overgrown and inaccessible, for gardening was not one of his hobbies. Nor was cooking, one of the most popular of pastimes, and there is a good reason for this. Finally he resolved to find a brand new hobby, something overwhelming.

He settled on cloud farming. It was a perfect choice. For one thing, to the best of his knowledge, nobody in history had been a cloud farmer, so it wouldn't be possible for him to embarrass himself when asked what his job was. "I'm a cloud farmer," he would say, and the conversation would be over, and he could sneer with absolute contempt at anyone who hoped to contradict him directly or elicit more details in the hope of tripping him up. His sneer would strongly imply that discussing the subject further was beneath him, that cloud farmers never stooped so low, that ordinary folks simply had no need to know more about the occupation of cloud farming. At parties he would henceforth be secure, his anxiety levels would drop to bearable, and if he did do any writing it would be in secret at night. Not that Wilson went to many parties in the city.

But it's better to be safe than sorry, that's what the saying wants us to believe, which is odd when you think about it, because logically it means that if we insult someone we only need to take care crossing roads, avoid walking under ladders, and don't run with scissors, instead of offering an apology to the person we have offended. Anyway, Wilson invented cloud farming, in theory you can see him farming clouds every day of the week if you wish, and that is how he saved himself from the awful fate of being defined as a fiction writer in this fiction. I now suspect that cloud farming is mainly some purely mental exercise rather than a physical activity, but who am I to pass judgment on such things? Please don't assume that I am the author who put Wilson here and gave him his role as a writer. No, that author is fictional too, and I invented him. . . .

I ought to point out at this stage that the reason Wilson didn't cook his own food, or indeed eat anything at all, is because he was clockwork. He was a man, yes, it would be unfair to deny him that privilege, if privilege it truly is, but he was a clockwork man. I don't know why I am using the past tense. He still is a clockwork man. I wound him up this morning, for I'm one of his best friends and I often go to visit him. The fictional author that I created has turned the tables on me and put me as a character inside this story. But the last thing I want to be is a writer within a story, for the reasons already stated, and I beg Wilson to help me extricate myself from the situation. He offers to show me cloud farming, to teach the methods and madness that will enable me to become a cloud farmer too. I accept at once, but I insist on taking my oboe with me.

Because Wales receives so much rainfall it doesn't need while some other countries are at risk of drought, it was once decided that sharing the water would be a good idea. Giving the excess rainfall to arid lands by means of a long pipeline might seem to be highly impractical, but we must consider that the crude oil industry already has networks of such pipelines crossing continents and no one mocks them.

Accordingly, a pipeline of several thousand miles was constructed due south from a point on the western tip of Wales. It was totally straight, not for the sake of efficiency but because the engineers who designed it had a dislike of bends, and it spanned the sea and speared through the whole of Spain before crossing into Morocco, from whence it continued to traverse hunks of Algeria, Mauritania, Mali.

It stopped near the border with Burkina Faso, a country desperately in need of rain and here it disgorged the millions of gallons of water that had come so far without a passport. A pond expanded at this point and it soon became a pool and then a lake. Everything appeared to be working for the ultimate benefit of everyone. From now on Wales would be less saturated and Burkina would be more fertile. . . .

Some people wondered why a pipeline was necessary and whether an old-fashioned aqueduct wouldn't have done the trick just as well, saving on materials. But the engineers answered that an open aqueduct would be clogged with seagulls and all sorts of unspecified rubbish within a year. A fully enclosed pipeline was much better. And this act of foresight brought its own tragedy, as you shall now hear.

A few daring citizens of Wales, fed up to the sodden back teeth with a life of ceaseless pounding rain, saw an opportunity for an easy escape to a sunnier realm. Furthermore, the trip would require no expensive aeroplane ticket and no complicated visa. They could simply utilize the pipeline as a water chute and ride it to dryness! They made their way to the western tip of the nation where the pipeline began.

Despite their big lungs they wouldn't be able to hold their breath quite as long as the voyage would take; but there was an answer to this breathy objection in the form of scuba gear. The few daring citizens put on diving suits and jumped into the mouth of the pipeline and allowed the current of the rain to convey them contentedly to Africa, where they emerged after a few days with a joyful splash in a lake.

The success of the pioneers encouraged others to make the journey. It wasn't long before half the population of Wales was jostling at the mouth of the pipeline, keen to be carried smoothly and cleanly for free to a place where a cloud is a treat rather than an oppressor. One by one they jumped in and were accelerated down the conduit. But now we come to a delicate matter that isn't very pleasant to discuss.

But the issue can't be avoided. The fact is that many Welsh people are overweight. They drink too much beer and stuff their faces with too many pies and chips. This isn't a value judgment but an objective statement that has a vital bearing on the history of the pipeline. Let us remind ourselves that everybody, no matter what size or shape, has equal rights! Good. It is important to be utterly lucid about this.

Anyway, the fatties caused the disaster. They were just too large to fit and they got stuck. It only takes one clot to clog an artery. Then there was an almighty jam of tubbies, a steadily mounting backlog of blubberlings, and the pipeline was blocked. The flow of precious rainwater from Wales to Africa abruptly ceased. Any passenger who now leaped into the mouth of the pipeline was committing suicide.

But they continued to jump in, making the blockage even worse, and I felt a pang in my heart for them. So desperate were they to escape the rain that they didn't even care about dying horribly from slow asphyxiation in a long tubular coffin far from home. They were like little creatures that a snake has swallowed. They were digested inside their own diving suits. It was a grotesque end for brave travellers.

The pipeline had been constructed from some transparent material. So it was often possible to observe the decaying bodies of the stuck men and women, like stodge in a gut, with their empty oxygen cylinders and rictus grins. One of them, I noticed, had even taken a book with him to read on the way. *The Key in my Back* by Wilson the Clockwork Man. But he had only got to chapter two. A small mercy.

It certainly is wrong to make fun of fat people. I declined to laugh when a very fat man got on the bus a few weeks ago. It was the coach that travels from London to Swansea, briefly pausing at Bristol, Newport and Cardiff on the way. This bus is the cheapest method of commuting between these locations and is often uncomfortably packed as a consequence; but on this occasion I was the only passenger and thus looking forward to a peaceful journey without screaming children or canoodling couples disturbing me. Then the fat man got on. I had seen fat men before who had taken up two seats rather than one with their girth.

But this fellow was so enormous he took up more than two seats. It's no exaggeration to say that he took up *all* the seats downstairs. The bus is a double-decker, so I relocated upstairs. Then his wife, who I hadn't seen until now because he eclipsed her, got on. There was no space downstairs for her so she came upstairs too. Needless to say I had to spend the trip on the roof of the bus and in fact so did the driver. The bus had to drive itself for once. It was windy and cold up there. They were the fattest folks I've ever seen. I suppose they were returning to Wales on a pie and chips fact-finding mission. I didn't laugh once.

Fictional stories rely on very unnatural conventions in order to create the illusion of reality. A new character is introduced into the text, and no matter how hectic and urgent the action, the author will pause to describe him or her, even if just briefly, rather than allowing them to rush in, do what they must, and then depart for the next task. This pause is aberrant, ridiculous and offends truth, or so said Wilson to me once, and he should know because he has been an author.

And yet it does happen in real life! At least it does in Wales. Where I live, every time a new person enters the room they stop on the threshold and say slowly, "I am of middling height, with brown hair and blue eyes. My posture betrays the fact I work with crates of potatoes but also enjoy a round of golf on Sundays. Cloud farming is only a hobby, not a real job. My beard bristles when I pass electricity substations. . . ." and only then do they enter the room fully. Every time!

I don't want this text to be like that. The fat man and his wife on the bus were just ciphers, focal points around which an incident happened. The incident, if anything, was the real character. The couple got on the bus without giving me time to see them as people that can be described. I just was aware of two bulks without much definition. I travel on that bus frequently. I am a regular. But on principle I don't intend to permit any description of myself to appear here.

Wilson is the only clockwork man I know who won't give you the time of day. Not that he is unfriendly. He doesn't wear a watch. He prefers to tell the time by the slow passage of the sun across the sky. In Wales this can't be done, so Wilson will always change the subject if you ask him for the time. He will talk ethics instead, or maybe quantum theory. Or he will ask me to play a melody on the oboe.

The clouds are curtains drawn over the face of the sky in Wales. The last person to view the sun here was a Dutch tourist who was so tall his upper half poked above the level of the clouds and he went home telling everyone who would listen that it never rains in Wales, that the stories are untrue, but that something kept making his legs wet. He assumed sheep had been urinating against his legs.

That was the logical deduction for him. He lived the rest of his tall life believing that sheep are evil. He even wrote a poem on the theme. Wilson thought it was an awful poem, but that might be a jealous reaction. You know what writers are like; and even though Wilson is a cloud farmer he is still a writer deep in his brass psychology. Syntax bothers him and so do grammar and the Oxford comma.

I
have no
desire to lambast
sheep but ewe forced me to
with your woolly
thinking about
rams

They start fires on ships
and sink them to the bottom of the sea
deliberately so that
giant clams can bite the hulls

They incite riots among gulls
and encourage them to peck spinsters
at funerals and elevenses
and during each long pause on tours

Rams
do things like
that every day because
they think they are
above the
law

This is why I must disagree
when you state that all sheep are nice
and never fleece passersby
and always vote for peace, not war
because this is what you heard

If you had only seen what I saw
when I visited Wales . . .

[30]

A man was out at night walking his shadow. He walked it in the light of the yellow streetlamps that bathed the street in the centre of the city. The shadow was long and folded itself whenever it touched a wall, no matter what material that wall was made from, as if marking the page of a book with a dog-ear. But it was its own page.

The man kept pausing to allow his shadow to sniff at the surfaces that it was cast upon. It was very late and not many people were out. Only the shadow walkers prevented the city from being lifeless, and no doubt they too would have preferred to be home, but shadows need regular exercise no matter how tired their owners may be.

Other walkers brought their own shadows along and they too stopped where previous shadows had been. I was on the bus at the time, travelling from London to Swansea, and we were now passing through the centre of Cardiff. It had been a slow, uncomfortable journey and most of the other passengers were asleep. But I was awake.

I wondered what those other passengers would see if they awoke and looked out of the windows of the bus too. Probably they would see weary old men unable to walk without taking rests every dozen steps or so. But I didn't want to see it that way. I wanted to see shadow walkers exercising their shadows, shadows of diverse forms.

One of the walls of Cardiff Castle is topped with statues of beasts. If a hand held to a light a certain way can make the shadow of a rabbit, what parts of our anatomy suitably twisted will make such a range of animals? Had the shadows of ancient walkers snapped off while sniffing that wall and over long ages petrified into sculpture?

The wall of animals particularly fascinated me when I was young. I found the pelican to be incongruous, thus comical. Positioned among lions and hyenas, it seemed tame and absurd. I didn't realise that in heraldic terms the pelican is no less valid a device than more glamorous and dangerous creatures. Also that pelicans can be vicious.

When I was a student there was a brief fashion of giving the pelican a hat. I remember seeing it wearing a sombrero, but only a cheap version of that noble headgear. Another time it sported a spotted handkerchief like a pirate. Its expression did seem to alter depending on what it wore. Often it looked smug, sometimes a little astounded.

Someone broke off the nose of the anteater and attention was diverted away from the pelican to this even more absurd statue that had somehow escaped our scrutiny. It was fixed later with a stone nose that was slightly different in colour. I saw it crawling with ants on a wet summer day. A stone anteater shouldn't be humiliated in this fashion, I reflected to myself, but only much later, this very morning in fact. . . .

It was recently my fiftieth birthday. I have been alive for half a century. This fact, while unremarkable in itself, continues to astonish me when I stand before the mirror. I see the reflection of a man who is also fifty years old. Between us we have lived a full century.

Yet this man isn't a different man to me. He is me and I am him. His fifty years can be added to my own. The sum is easy and produces a total of one hundred years, a full century. His years are mine too; they belong to me. I don't see how I can reject them.

So I have reached the grand old age of one hundred, at least when I am in front of a mirror, and thus I'm entitled to a telegram of congratulation from the Queen. That's the tradition; and the Queen was alive the first time I stood in front of the mirror and doubled my age just like that. Has she forgotten me? Has her telegram been intercepted?

I can't bear the thought that I am an unacknowledged centenarian. My wrath is directed at my reflection, who has done this thing to me, and so I reach out to clutch him by the throat. He also reaches out to clutch me by the throat. Our hands meet on the surface.

The mirror is knocked from the wall. It was hanging there on a piece of string looped around a nail driven into the wall. The mirror falls down but doesn't break on the carpet, thank goodness, and something else falls with it. Something that has been hiding behind the mirror. A telegram. It must have been put there by royal decree.

I pick it up and read it, and this is what it says:

"A big bus will seat fifty passengers. Fifty copies of you are equal to two and a half thousand years of history. These copies can be made. A bus full of mirrors awaits you outside. I want you to get on it now and go all the way to Ancient Egypt to find out the true secret of mummification. I'm sure they've been keeping something back. I am your queen and this is my command. Oh yes, happy birthday."

People obsessed by the Oxford comma need to spend time in Cambridge, Harvard, and the Sorbonne.

If the Tempus ain't broken don't Fugit.

People tell him that he has a "crooked smile" and it's true, he does. His smile embezzled one hundred doubloons from the East India Company in 1639.

Be like a tree, the Guru told him. It's the best way to be. But he is already like a tree. He has nuts.

The first story he published was about a man employed by Hitler to run around with a cushion to ensure that Nazi pilots with failed parachutes had soft landings. It was called 'The Catcher in the Reich'.

The roses that cover those little grey houses in the rain are trying to get inside and be dry, he insists. But it sometimes rains indoors in Wales too, especially if you keep sheep in the attic.

The rain in Spain falls mainly on the plane. The rain in Wales falls on all vehicles equally.

Beach umbrellas in Wales are in fact local people who have evolved to cope with the rain. Sitting under one is the equivalent of sitting under a stranger and might be considered improper.

(These are a few observations pertinent to Wilson the Clockwork Man. I know he'll appreciate them. His nuts are brass, by the way, the doubloons were gold, and the cushion was floral.)

I have already discussed the fact that it's an exaggeration to say that the rain never stops in Wales. But an exaggeration often gets to the core of an experience more effectively and honestly than a statement of truth. If I am going to be strictly accurate, I can assert that it rains in Wales on an average of 320 days out of 365. Are the people supposed to be grateful for those measly 45 days of dryness? Well, they aren't. And the best way to convey their indignation, which in my view is justified, is to maintain that it rains every single day.

Now I am in a position to apply some logic. The best position for the application of logic, I have found, is legs akimbo. If it rains every single day in Wales, the solution is for the days to no longer be single. The best course of action is therefore to introduce them to other single days in the hope they will pair up and form couples. This might break the pattern of rain, the hellish and abominable pattern of everlasting rain. Let's see what happens if we arrange a blind date between (for example) January 4th and August 19th. How will they get along?

Unfortunately it turns out that attraction between days largely depends on which *year* those days come from. January 4th last year might have lots in common with August 19th from ten years ago but nothing at all with an updated version. Arranging dates between dates turns out to be a science. Let's keep trying. Romance blossoms in the most unlikely ways. At least there is a notable success. Who could have imagined that June 12th in the 25th Century AD would have been such a perfect match for December 2nd 1253 BC? They are going to get married.

The clouds attend and throw confetti as the happy couple came out of the holy wormhole. They throw the only confetti they can throw, colossal raindrops that act like prisms; and those prisms create Welsh rainbows, an arc of monochrome bands, each a slightly gloomier shade of grey. There are no pots of gold at the ends of Welsh rainbows. There are only pots of cold stagnant soup made from rain-mashed chips and pies, and no spoons to eat it with, only strands of seaweed vaguely resembling cutlery. That's Wales for you. Why not come and visit?

In every other country of the world there is a clear separation between sea and land. The surface of the sea is a geometrical entity. It divides the two worlds cleanly, even if not smoothly, the upper and lower realms, the dry and watery biospheres. But in Wales the divide is not obvious, it is fuzzy, and this fuzziness comes from the fact that it rains so heavily and unceasingly, so the sky contains more water than air.

Fish that rise to the surface of the sea get confused. On the coastlines of other nations, the fish stop because they can go no further. But around the shores of Wales, the rain is so thick that the fish can rise up into it and swim into the sky. Then winds will blow them ashore, but they are alive and still swimming through the rain. They will enter cities in shoals and be quite content to negotiate the streets.

Flying fish generally have wings, but not in Wales. They fly because they believe they are still swimming. If you venture out into the public spaces of Cardiff or Swansea, you are highly likely to be slapped in the face by a cod. And it's not just fish. Crabs, giant clams, dolphins, octopi and even walruses can be found drifting about. There is a story that once a mermaid did the same thing. Maybe so.

Once I saw a blue whale, a sperm whale and The White Whale taking it in joyful turns to go the wrong way down a one-way street. The rascally cetaceans! That is Wales for you and is how the country earned its name in the first place. Wilson told me this and I believe him utterly. He added that rain-drenched fish are far more slippery than margarine and I believe him butterly. Believing Wilson is my task.

So I am on my way to Ancient Egypt because I don't dare to disobey the Queen's instructions. To get there I need a good excuse for the customs officers at the entrance to the holy wormhole. I told them I am going to check out the eligibility of a certain day in the year 526 BC as a possible wife for a nice modern Welsh day. They accept this and wave through the bus I'm travelling on, a bus full of dozens of my own reflections seated in mirrors. The bluff has made me uneasy.

I try reading a book to distract my mind, *Key Insights* by Wilson, but it just isn't my thing. I wonder how I will be greeted in Ancient Egypt? It is likely the Pharoah will be annoyed by my presence and do cruel things to me. I wish the Queen would leave me alone. I wish she would bugger off. The Queen is mean. I have never given her orders, so why should she boss me around just because she has an idea that I am one hundred years old? This is harassment of senior citizens, I insist.

Then it occurs to me that if the bus is full of copies of my reflection, how can I be sure that I am the real me? I might be one of the duplicated images. If so, there's no need for me to go along, they won't miss one of so many reflections. When the driver stops for a rest and lets us all off to stretch our legs for a few minutes, I quietly slip away. We are halfway to Ancient Egypt in time and space, probably somewhere in the vicinity of Roman Italy, and I am facing a long hike.

I know in my heart of hearts (and considering the number of copies of me on this trip the cliché is accurate) that I am probably the real me, but I console, embolden and justify myself with the possibility that maybe I'm just a flat image on an oblong of silvered glass. How can forest thorns or lightning storms injure an image? I proceed with a loping gait, a gait I've always been fond of despite the fact it squeaks and needs oiling. I usually keep it unlocked, that loping gait of mine.

I enter a forest and step on dry twigs, a luxury unheard of in Wales. It is music to my ears, partly because it can't really be music to my nose or tongue or anything *other* than my ears, partly because these twigs appear to be tuned. As I hasten between the trees, the years slip off me like satin shackles. Then the twigs begin to make less and less noise underfoot and the ground between the twigs makes more and more. It squelches. Now I know I'm finally nearing the Welsh border.

The forests of Wales are full of strange and unexpected creatures. All are damp and many are semi-aquatic. There is the bogbunny, the flatypus, the squelcher and the puddlesnake. None are venomous but most are cold and clammy. There are also more conventional beasts: pumas, aardvarks, wolves and toads. Innumerable brooks and streams and tributaries make a complicated pattern on the ground, a pattern that if seen from above looks just like the face of an enraged old monarch.

But who views the forest from above? Birds in Wales fly upside down in order to prevent the napes of their necks getting wet. It's not a country for birds. It's the only one in the world where a phoenix can't burn itself to death without being put out first. No one can say exactly what enraged old monarch is depicted by the traceries of flowing water. Some of these streams can be jumped easily, but others are too wide. At one point I am forced to utilise a snoring grizzly as a bridge.

We all have our bears to cross. This one straddled a river when it fell asleep. I wake it up by the act of stepping on it. Up it rises with a roar and I am forced to defend myself with a pointed stick. The tip of the stick rips the skin of the bear. Turns out it's just a cheap bear costume instead of an authentic beast. As the costume disintegrates I see that the Queen is hiding inside, growling and craving honey. Her face is identical to the pattern of streams seen from above. Her crown glistens.

I am in trouble now. She first lectures me on my failings as one of her subjects, then lists the punishments I deserve for letting her down. She is shaking her fist in my direction. There is only one course of action for me to take. I hurl Wilson's book at her. It knocks the crown off her head and into the bushes. She lets out a cry of horrified anguish and jumps into the undergrowth in order to find it. I make my escape the same way I make a mug of tea, while Her Majesty isn't watching.

And is my escape successful? I will answer that question with another question, two questions in fact. Does the Pope shit in the woods? Is a bear a Catholic? In other words, I'm not sure. I will let you know when I know the answer myself. The word 'success' has an unclear definition in Wales and one mustn't be hasty to celebrate anything here. I pause for breath. I don't think the Queen is chasing me now, but this doesn't mean I'm safe. She has spies, assassins, retainers everywhere.

The Dutch tourist who was taller than the clouds and who despised sheep was called Van der Graaf and he died in very mysterious circumstances in his apartment in Rotterdam. He had been strangled but there was no sign of any break-in and no fingerprints of any intruders, no forensic evidence at all. He had been strangled with his own scarf. The police investigators attached no significance to the fact the scarf was woollen. Who can blame them? They were Dutch, not Welsh.

It was officially required that a post-mortem be performed on Van der Graaf and it was found, quite oddly, that his heart was shaped exactly like the chess piece called a pawn. This has nothing to do with his death. Why should a man by the name of Van der Graaf have a pawn heart? Nobody knows why, nobody, not my body, not his body, not even the body of the police force tasked with investigating the crime. It is just so. Truly this is a strange world full of peculiarities.

While we are on the subject of pawns, it might be worthwhile pointing out that Welsh men dance like chess pieces. Not just pawns but rooks and bishops and knights, sometimes even kings, but very rarely queens. They move rigidly on the dancefloor according to the rules, from one square to another, seeking to checkmate. They lack fluidity, which is ironic when it is remembered how much fluid they are drenched with every day of their lives. But perhaps that's the answer.

They are doing their best to oppose fluidity, to hope that stiffness and dryness will one day evolve into synonyms. Their dancing is a gesture of defiance against the rain. In the sickly lamps of the dancehalls their faces shine with the effort of concentration. But the rain will not be denied its little victory. Sweat pours from the pores of the dancing men, sweat that is the cousin and friend of the rain, and it drips onto the floor like a salty spring shower, an indoor downpour.

"When you're strange, faces come out of the rain," sang Jim Morrison. But in Wales it's not necessary to be strange to achieve this effect. The faces have no choice.

Please don't be left with the erroneous impression that poor dead Van der Graaf is the only foreigner to have visited Wales in my lifetime or in the lifetimes of other characters mentioned in these pages. Wales has hosted a large number of people from many lands in the course of its history. One of these immigrants may be in a position to tell you exactly *how* many. I am speaking of none other than Karl Mondaugen, the mad scientist from Munich, who currently lives in Cardiff.

As well as being a mathematical genius, Mondaugen is the finest and most prolific inventor ever to grace these shores. He once developed the perfect tranquilliser in order to catch a mouse that kept raiding his kitchen and he delivered this formidable substance via a dart and peashooter. The creature instantly fell into a profound slumber and Mondaugen picked it up by the tail and relocated it to a spot in the forest a mile from his home. This seemed the most humane method.

But the tranquilliser was just too good. A cat that came along ate the mouse and also fell asleep; then a wandering dog ate the cat; a puma ate the dog; a puddlesnake swallowed the puma whole; a squelcher ingested the puddlesnake; then a flatypus chomped the squelcher; a bogbunny in the vicinity consumed the flatypus; and it got even worse than this. The tranquilliser simply wouldn't wear off. It was too powerful, too perfect. A week later Mondaugen went for a stroll.

He found the forest path blocked by an immense bloated shape. It was a sleeping mountain, a very rare flesh mountain that had just happened to come along and find an unconscious ballyhoo. There's nothing rare flesh mountains like more than ballyhoos, so naturally it had it for lunch. But inside the ballyhoo was a diminishing series of drugged meals, including the shlurper the ballyhoo had eaten, the gamoth devoured by the shlurper, the hunky munched by the gamoth, the zigydoodo and so on, all the way to the flatypus and ultimately the mouse.

Mondaugen wasn't daunted. He is never daunted. Nothing stops him from inventing things; and it is widely rumoured that Wilson was one of his early efforts, although a few original thinkers claim it was vice versa and that M is simply an epiphenomenon, animus or inversion of W. These obscure arguments don't interest me. But Mondaugen's actual inventions always astound. One of his many creations was a genetically engineered millipede-toucan hybrid and when he first announced the concept to me my only question was: who foots the bill?

Perhaps my favourite Mondaugen project was the land submarine he designed to make life easier for those who wished to travel around Wales. The prototype was shaped like a rhino and was devoured by a zigydoodo one morning in the fog. The next models were in the form of whales, blue whales, sperm whales and The White Whale and these were much better subs in every way. Nothing came to eat them. Not successfully anyway. A few krakens tried but failed miserably.

I owned one myself and I took it to pay a call on Wilson. He watched it swim through the rain towards his flock of clouds. His expression was dour at first, then determined, and he raised his crook to point it at me. A bolt of energy spurted from the end and struck the hull of my sub. All the workings seized up and my whale clattered to a halt. I threw open the iron hatch and clambered out, my hair crackling with static. I never knew until that very instant that Wilson was armed.

"You were spooking my clouds," he explained.

I apologized and he also said sorry. Then he told me a tale about how a philosopher had once tried to worry his entire flock by preaching ethical nihilism to it. He had been forced to pick that fellow up and hurl him like a metaphysical spear all the way back to where he'd come from, possibly England or somewhere like that. A clockwork man is strong enough to do this. It had made Wilson more defensive.

"I understand you care for every single cloud," I said.

"They are my children," he replied.

"You are a good entity."

"Take that one, for example," he said, indicating a very fine specimen of a very high cloud. "It's a boy and he really was my child, my only son and heir. Don't be surprised that a clockwork man can have children! The clue is the word 'spring' in offspring."

"But he's a cloud now! What happened to him?"

"He ran off to join the cirrus."

"Well, you can't hold onto them forever."

"True, true," he sighed.

"Mondaugen is *your* father," I ventured.

He didn't take the bait. While waiting for his crook to recharge he just muttered inanities, then suddenly he asked, "What is the mad scientist up to these days? Apart from submarines."

"Invisible men," I said.

Wilson shook his head. "They won't work."

"I know," I concurred.

"Not in Wales, they won't. Invisible men are only right for dry lands. An invisible man will be plain to see in the Welsh rains, like a bubble of air walking down the street. An invisible man here would be easier to see than a visible man. That's Wales for you."

"He's breeding them for a very specific purpose."

"Tell me," urged Wilson.

I relished an opportunity to talk without drowning. It was one of those uncommon dry days in the year and it was a pleasure to open my mouth wide without feeling it fill with cold water. In Wales people speak to each other through mouths so slitted, for fear of inundating them, that postmen, half blinded by the rain in their eyes, often attempt to push sodden letters through them, mistaking them for doors.

"An invisible man is one who reflects no light," I began. "In fact light passes straight through him without distortion. If there were distortion he wouldn't be invisible. We would notice that something was amiss and he would be rumbled. He would be merely a transparent man. So then! An authentic invisible man is one who distorts the passage of light even less than air does. Now imagine a queue made up entirely of invisible men. It is a very long queue at the bank and it is perfectly straight. If you stood at the back of this queue, you would have a clearer view of the counter and the cashier than if the invisible men weren't there. The longer the queue, the more noticeable the difference!"

"I don't have a bank account. I am clockwork."

"It's a hypothetical situation, my friend. Mondaugen wants to breed and rent out invisible men to surveyors and astronomers. Invisible men stacked together in horizontal or vertical lines will cut out the distortions and aberrations that air, which has density and also tends to move, creates between the observer and observed."

"He plans a tower of invisible men all the way to the moon? But they will die in the vacuum of space. . . ."

"Only the ones at the base will be human," I said.

"And the others?"

"Clockwork."

"Just like me," he sighed.

"Just, as you say, like you. This is what he is working on at present. I answered because you asked me."

Wilson nodded somberly. His crook had fully charged now and it was clear he wanted to change the subject. He frowned his brass eyebrows in my direction and after the tiny echoes of the clash had faded, he invited me to explain why I travelled everywhere with an oboe. It was something he'd long been curious about, but it had never seemed an appropriate time to bring up the subject. Why an oboe?

In fact there's nothing special about my oboe. It could be a bassoon, tuba, trombone or any instrument played with the mouth. The reason it is an oboe and I carry it with me on my travels is because it fits the vulcanite case I have, whereas the others don't.

It's that simple. But I suspect you want a fuller explanation than this. Wilson certainly wasn't satisfied with that reply. Why an instrument of any kind, he insisted on knowing? I've nothing to be ashamed of. I told him the truth. It was part of a strategy.

The Pied Piper cast a melodic lure on rats and led them away from the town they were plaguing. My dream is to be an Odd Oboist and weave an aural spell on the clouds. I hope to lead them away from Wales, over hills and through valleys, and maybe into the mouth of a cave where they will become lost in extensive subterranean labyrinths of rock. To achieve this, it is required that I play the oboe well.

That's putting it lightly. I need to play the oboe better than anyone has played it before; or rather I must learn how to appeal irresistibly to clouds with oboe music, to mesmerize and misguide them, to trick them and turn Wales into a land where the rain stopped. It's imperative that I discover if a melody exists that clouds can't resist.

That's why I travel, seeking that speculative tune, which may not exist and not be playable even if it does. So I scrutinize ancient musical scores in dusty libraries and university archives; and I consult bearded yokels in obscure inns who dimly recall that their father's mother's uncle knew a man who played the hurdy-gurdy in a storm and the storm followed him and then he jumped in a well and they went in too and now the reflection at the bottom of the well shows those particular clouds even when the sky above is dotted with quite different ones.

In other words I want to rescue Wales! I want to make it a drier place than it is. Wilson is unimpressed with me and he grits teeth of bronze and tin and sloshes acidic spittle around them, as if hoping to boost the power of his indignation with a mouthful of improvised batteries. I am prepared for his rebuke when it finally comes:

"Clouds are my livelihood. I am a cloud farmer."

"You're a writer," I retort.

"Not in this story, I'm not! I hate stories about writers. I refuse to be one. I am a cloud farmer and that's that! If you ever learn to play the tune you seek, you will be guilty of cloud stealing. Our friendship will be over on that day, I warn you, and I'll come after you and discharge my crook into you without mercy and fry you."

"Why do the Welsh insist on frying everything?"

"My crook doesn't grill or bake, even though that would be healthier. Besides, I don't want revenge on you to be healthy. Quite the opposite! I want you to suffer. It's best we don't speak of this anymore. Clouds are like family to me. I'll protect them."

"You aren't the only one who is after my blood."

"Yes, the Queen hates you!"

"If the Queen destroys me, you will be denied vengeance."

"I will protect you from the Queen!"

"In order to kill me yourself?"

"Indeed, my friend!"

Wilson is deadly serious and I drop the subject. We are standing on a hill and the dropped subject rolls down the slope, gaining speed, turning into a blur, until it strikes the side of my sub. The impact does something to its inner workings and suddenly the vehicle is operational again. I bid farewell to the clockwork man and clamber through the hatch, sit on the pilot's cushion and steer it back home.

It trundles on squeaky auxiliary wheels until the rains come again and it can swim through the moisture, lashing its tail and projecting fountains of water through its blowhole. On the way back I am overtaken on a road by a car and one of the passengers opens a window and hurls a harpoon at me, which deflects harmlessly off my iron hull. Bloody students! Do they really have nothing better to do today?

The comparison between sheep and clouds that I've insisted upon making in these pages can be regarded as a whimsical and unoriginal conceit that has a childish element about it. Clouds and sheep aren't the same thing, though I have previously stated that they are; which serves to demonstrate merely the paucity and immaturity of my imagination. Clouds and sheep belong to different categories of objects and comparing them is as futile as trying to compare apples and oranges.

This is a typical objection that critics might make against me. Yet I regard such a protest as invalid. I *have* compared apples and oranges in my lifetime, quite successfully too, and I can even do so right now. In front of me in a bowl I have an apple and an orange. The apple is green, the orange is orange. The apple is smaller than the orange and lighter. I will peel the orange but not the apple. I might play tennis with the apple but not the orange. They can be compared!

They are both examples of fruit. That is their connection. This is how I'm able to regard them as identical items. That one is a fruit, that other one is also a fruit. It's the same with sheep and clouds. Quite aside from the fact that sheep have rained on me, I'm only required to refer to both as 'aspects of Wales' for them to achieve total equivalence. Sheep are an aspect of Wales; clouds are an aspect of Wales. They are thus identical. I perceive no flaw at all in this simple logic.

> "Then I looked at the window and thought: why, yes, it's just the rain, the rain, always the rain, and turned over, sadder still, and fumbled about for my dripping sleep and tried to slip it back on."
>
> (Ray Bradbury)

Mondaugen designed the bus that can seat eighty passengers. It is circular in shape and every passenger gets a window to peer out of. A problem is that it takes up the entire highway and the rim of its circumference tends to protrude over the verge into whatever borders the road, so it has been known to trim hedges as it glides along country lanes. Mondaugen drew the original plans on a round beer mat. He didn't have a pen or pencil on him at the time so he just submitted the mat to the patents office. It went into production a few days later but only one model was sold. The Queen bought it and nobody knows why. Mondaugen regards the vehicle as just another in his series of land submarines modelled on ocean creatures. The circular bus is a jellyfish, he maintains.

The bus had no seat numbered 13. This is the same as Spanish planes, on which the rain mainly falls. They don't have seats numbered 13 either. In Italy the situation is the same. No seat 13. For a long time I couldn't see what bad luck a person in seat 13 on a plane could have that wouldn't be equally unlucky for those in seats 12 and 14. Then I caught a plane from Wales to Spain and discovered the answer.

It was a Welsh plane, so it had a seat numbered 13, and I was seated on it. Next to me, on seat 12, was a very obnoxious man; and next to me on the other side, on seat 14, was another very obnoxious man. And now I knew what that bad luck could be, the bad luck on a plane that would affect a passenger on seat 13 but not fellow passengers on seats 12 and 14. The bad luck was the quality of the passengers.

I was travelling because I'd heard a rumour that the clouds that floated in the sky above the little city of Albarracín in Aragon, an especially remote region, could be made to sway back and forth in the sky by music. A harp player was said to do this once a month, parking her harp on the summit of a peak and plucking an old dance tune.

It might be nice to convert the raw data of rainfall in Wales into graphical form. What better method to do this than with a pie chart? Pies are very popular in this country as appetizers to meals that consist of pies followed by pies for dessert, not forgetting the chips as a side dish and the beer that washes it all down while eternal rain washes colour out of the sky and out of our lives with equal meticulousness.

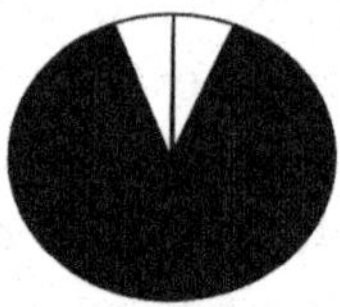

The pie represents an average Welsh year; the black area is the days on which rain never stops falling. The white area depicts those days that are dry or relatively dry. Curiously enough the shape given here is the same shape as the raindrops themselves.

It is true. Each raindrop is circular and oily with a clear wedge near its top. This clear wedge acts like a prism and is responsible for generating the grey rainbows that arc like concrete bridges over the industrial wastes of certain valleys in the south of the country. When light passes through the prisms the rainbows totter precariously out of thin air and indicate the locations of crocks of foul and lethal soup.

Meteorologists dread being sent to Wales to work.

Every year an area equal to the size of Wales is rained on in Wales.

I know what you're thinking. Every four years there is an extra day in the year and the chart doesn't indicate what happens on that day. Does it rain or is it dry? February 29th is the only day when it's possible to write a rain cheque successfully in Wales. That's the answer to the question. It is also the only day when one can escape the sheer misery of the rain by using a pair of homemade wings. Yes it is.

If something is 'sheer' it is either translucent or else it is like a cliff. In this case the latter meaning applies. One can strap on the wings and jump off that sheer misery and maybe eventually land safely in warmer climes. When people in Wales say that they are "all in a flap" they are promising in public to make an escape attempt next leap year. The wings are usually made from balsa wood and plastic.

Had Icarus made his own journey with homemade wings in Wales he would have survived the flight. He was warned not to fly too close to the sun. In Wales there is no sun to fly too close to. But he wouldn't have had the name Icarus if he had really been Welsh. He would have been called something more along the lines of Ivor the Beak or Birdman Boyo. That's Wales for you. That's always Wales.

It's rare that the rain in Wales falls vertically the way rain ought to fall. It most commonly falls at an oblique angle. It's the wind that likes to make these angles. Welsh winds consider themselves to be clever at geometry and they are big cold show-offs. Sometimes the angle is so oblique that it is horizontal to the ground and the rain falls sideways. No umbrella ever invented can cope with such rainfall.

Sideways rain is one of the special symbols of Wales just like dragons and daffodils and long green onions. Rich people who can afford strong umbrellas can sometimes be seen sliding down the streets like ships, the umbrellas dragging them like mainsails to unknown destinations. Poorer people must rely on standard umbrellas, which turn inside out very easily and make the users look ridiculous.

Mondaugen once designed a windproof umbrella that wouldn't turn inside out no matter how hard the wind blew. Its canopy was formed of overlapping fabric leaves that fluttered in one direction only. When the rain falls on them, the leaves resist the assault; when the wind comes up under the canopy, the leaves open and allow it to pass through. For some reason the invention never caught on.

I once told the wind to "fuck off" but then I realised that all winds already are in the process of doing exactly that, which is the actual problem. It is not like me to swear, by the way. Begging the wind to "stay", like a dog, might be more effective. Windmills might be annoyed by that option, but that's their lookout. On the other hand, lookouts would have a better time of it without strong winds to batter them.

I also once told the clouds to "piss off" but then I realised that clouds are already doing exactly that. Again it's not normal for me to curse or use obscenities, but one reaches the end of one's tether. On the end of my tether was the key I had lost years ago. What was it doing there? It's the key to my attic, which has been locked a long time. I use this key to open the attic trapdoor and poke my head through.

A flock of clouds instantly stampedes over me; and every cloud rains on the crown of my head as it passes. I start thinking about the Queen and the crown of *her* head. If she wears a crown on her crown, does this mean she is greedy? Two crowns are more than enough for any monarch. Then I wonder how long the flock of clouds has been trapped up here? Perhaps they are vintage clouds and worth money.

Trying to insult the weather is ultimately as futile as trying to fight it. When I was young and living in the seaside town of Porthcawl, which is halfway between Cardiff and Swansea, a friend of mine suddenly flipped out. He could take no more of the endless rain and wind and he rushed off into the night before I could stop him, shaking his fist and challenging the weather to a fight. He was a brave fellow.

He returned maybe twenty minutes later, completely soaked, panting, his courage in sodden tatters around him, and he shrugged. "The weather won," he said simply. His shrug made a distinctive noise, the same noise as a grapefruit cut in half and rubbed against a windowpane. These clouds in my attic are possibly the same ones he fought back then. At least they might be relatives of them. Who knows?

I fetch my oboe and return to test out my latest melody on the rascals. It has no effect at all. I close the trapdoor and decide to invite an antiques dealer around to view them. He will give me an estimate of their value. I don't imagine they'll fetch much, but it's worth finding out for definite. I know a reliable antiques dealer by the name of Fiddly Buttons who deals in furniture rather than gloomy cumulus formations, but he's flexible. His spine is rubber. Mondaugen invented him.

If you don't believe any of this, allow me to insist that the part about my friend fighting the weather is absolutely true. His name was Ian Hewston and I haven't seen him for thirty years. Hand on heart, it really happened. As for the rest of it, maybe you should consider suspending your disbelief for your own sake if not for mine too.

I'm suspending my own disbelief right now, in order to preserve it for winter. Once it is dry, although nothing in Wales is ever completely so, I will take it down and smoke it in front of the fire. Then I will roll it in salt and seal it in a clean pickle jar. It's never too early in the year to suspend your disbelief. You'll need it throughout the coldest months, so it's good to have a ready supply. Believe me . . .

When in Rome do as the Romans do. That's the familiar saying. Who am I to dispute it or any other maxim? But the Romans did a lot of things in their history. Is one individual really supposed to replicate all that striving and expansion? I caught a flight from London to Rome, my oboe tucked under my arm, and when I landed I recalled the saying. One of the many things the Romans did was to invade and occupy Britain. I figured that of all their achievements, this was one I could do easily enough or at least I could make an attempt. I didn't leave the airport but caught the next plane back to Britain. The saying had won.

The only maxim I have ever disputed was Hiram Maxim, the inventor of the machinegun. He told me not to pick my nose, but I insisted that it was better than letting nature choose one.

My wife was abducted by a Roman warrior with a net and a trident. I'm not married but it happened anyway.

"Gladiator?"

"No, he didn't eat her, he just took her away."

It's often a source of bafflement to people from outside Wales that I don't speak Welsh. I learned the language when I was at school and that's why I don't speak it now. The teacher was a very stuffy person, the classroom was a very stuffy classroom, and even though it rained constantly outside on the playground I had an intense urge to be out there, playing glistening marbles with my dripping comrades.

The teacher made no attempt to make the language interesting, in fact I'm willing to say the opposite was true and that plenty of effort went into making it boring. So in my mind Welsh has become indelibly associated with stuffiness. This is a pity but there isn't much I can do about it. When I lived in Spain and people asked me to speak Welsh I babbled nonsense, which seemed to satisfy them deeply.

I once wrote a page of gobbledygook in the guest book of a mountain cottage in Cantabria and was applauded for doing so. Spanish, however, I found to be an easy language to acquire. I assumed that all other tongues of the Iberian peninsular would be equally unproblematic. But then I went to Portugal and had a rude awakening.

The way I speak Portuguese is by talking Spanish but leaving out all vowels, slurring every appearance of the letter 's' and doing this with a mouthful of custard tart. That's my method. A different kind of stuffiness with the drawback of making one tubbier. The way I speak Spanish is by taking the custard tart out of my mouth.

The rudest awakening I ever had was when a winter storm flung open my bedroom window and the wind roared, "No, *you* fuck off!" as it came inside, and the cloud that came with it and rained all over me added, "No, *you* piss off!" That was a much ruder awakening than the discovery that Portuguese is more tricky than Spanish.

The Queen is clearly my enemy.

There's a famous saying, "My enemy's enemy is my friend," but this implies that "my friend's friend is my enemy." The Queen is my enemy, as I have already established. So the Queen is my friend's friend. Which of my friends is she friends with?

I must work out who and prevail upon them to ask her to leave me in peace. I am not one hundred years old. That was a mistake, a trick of the mirror. I am only fifty years old. . . .

It heartens me to say "only" in conjunction with "fifty years old." It makes me feel almost young again. The circular bus is still on its way to Egypt with all those reflections of me. I wonder if they'll find what they have been told to seek? The lost secrets of the art of mummification. And I wonder if they will bring it back?

If my friend's friend is my enemy, then I must learn who are the friends of my friend. Which friend? I doubt it matters. Let's take Wilson as our example. He is my friend. Therefore I am his friend. Therefore I am my friend's friend. But this means that I am my own enemy! Enemies battle each other and strive to gain victories over them. How can I gain victory over myself without losing the fight?

This logical conundrum is too much for me. I give up.

But wait! If I have given up, it means I have surrendered! And if I've surrendered, then the victory is mine!

Thank you, logic, you have always been a real friend.

The friend who might actually be my enemy could be Mondaugen, as I'm never sure how much of a boon he is and how much of a menace. Highly possible that the menace part is greater.

The other day he invented a vampire with fairy wings. I didn't stop to ask if it was biological or clockwork or electronic. I just crossed myself, though I'm not that kind of believer, and crossed the road. Vampires with fairy wings aren't quite as disturbing as those with bat wings, but I don't want to take chances. Garlic mushrooms are the best deterrent, he told me afterwards. I have them for dinner now.

I sometimes wonder if half the beasts that roam the Welsh forest were invented by Mondaugen and not by evolution? I certainly don't remember there being any flapgoons and chortleducks when I was young. So where did they come from, if not from his laboratory? I know for a fact that he's just created a new hybrid and released it.

He calls it a chipmunkey and describes it as a "fried holy locksmith", one third chip, one third monk, one third key. It can burrow in the ground and climb trees with equal dexterity and open any door in the world with a twist of its noggin. It is daftly amusing.

Not all his inventions based on creatures are malign or mischievous. One or two help to preserve life. For example, it suddenly occurred to him that when two slices of bread are dropped at the same time on opposite sides of the world, the entire planet briefly becomes a giant sandwich. Then he realised that tectonic plates are like slices of bread and that the world has in fact always been a sandwich. A sandwich for whom? There must be a cosmic picnicker out there somewhere.

To prevent the Earth from being eaten by this unimaginable entity, he invented a colossal artificial space wasp. There is nothing more effective at separating picnickers from their meals than wasps. The artificial space wasp flew up into the atmosphere and was never seen again. Presumably it chased away the cosmic picnicker. We have no way of knowing. Radio astronomers tracking the thing found the buzzing to be too excruciating to endure and abandoned their apparatus.

But the planet hasn't been eaten; so let's give Mondaugen the benefit of the doubt. As for tectonic zones, they have a lot on their plate, and it's entirely their fault. 'Plate' and 'fault' are the axes of that joke. These axes are of no use against fairy vampires but they might come in useful if the Queen bursts into your house. Off with her head! What shall we do with it when it's off? Dry it carefully, put it in a corner of the room and disguise it as a globe of the world. Then at night, when no one is looking, take two pieces of bread and make a sandwich. . . .

In Welsh forests when I was a boy, even pumas were scarce. Yes, they did exist, but one hardly ever saw them. We tended to dream more about big cats than actually frolic with them.

Lately I have reverted to using blankets instead of remaining faithful to my duvet. The reason for this is that I have two blankets, one with a leopard pattern, the other with a tiger pattern, and when I wake up after a restless night and see them tangled together it looks like there has been a great big catfight. This is most pleasing.

The bus full of mirrors has just reached Turkey. Despite the anachronism, it is personally welcomed into the country by Atatürk himself and by his son, Ataböy. Jokes don't bother about veracity. Veracity is a city named after Vera. It's not the capital of Turkey.

The Queen ordered a messenger to deliver an envelope to the Pope. The messenger set off on the long journey and was never tempted to open the envelope and read the message inside.

After months of hard travelling, the messenger reached the Pope, who opened the envelope and read the letter with a frown that grew deeper and deeper. Finally the Pope reached for a loaded musket that was by his side and pointed it at the messenger's head.

"Clearly you have received some bad news," said the messenger, "but I'm not responsible for what has happened, so don't shoot the messenger! I completed my given task, that's all."

Silently, but with a grim expression, the Pope handed the letter to the messenger, who began sweating as he read it. The message said, "Please shoot the messenger who delivers this to you."

The Pope pulled the trigger of the gun and it went off.

A Selection of Wilson's Favourite Sayings:

"Go ahead, shoot the messenger!"

"Inside every thin man there's a fat man crushed to death in an oubliette."

"I lost my tongue and was mute for a week. Then it turned up behind the sofa and I'm no longer silent. I always speak as I find."

"I think I'm suffering from premature reincarnation."

"Ad hominem, subtract homonym, multiply by womanym, the result is always worrying!"

"Quipcealment is the art of hiding behind wordplay. And yet, when a man is tired of Pundom he is tired of laugh."

"Who were the original copycats?"

"Only burn your bridges if you have a canoe and crumpets to toast."

"Wear your heart on your sleeve but not if it's an artificial heart shaped like a ship and you have a billowing sleeve."

"Are mad sentinels sentimental?"

"I am approximately in love, amour or less."

"I spent all morning trying to overtake a giant centipede but now I'm on the final leg of my journey."

"My father's brother's nephew's slobbering son is my spitting image."

"Just be yourself. If you are a fool, act like a fool. If you are an idiot, act like an idiot. Don't be afraid to be what you really are! If you are a fake, be an authentic fake. Don't be a phoney fake."

A way of escaping my obligations to the Queen that recently occurred to me is to argue that I am not actually fifty years old; therefore I am not a hundred years old in front of a mirror.

To do this convincingly, it is not enough to lie. The Queen would see through a simple deceit at once; and if she didn't, her retainers, assassins and spies would be sure to. I have to find a way of not being fifty that is true. I must really not be fifty somehow.

I listen to the rain on my windowpane. I am in bed, curled up around the springs that have poked through the sagging mattress. It is still only the afternoon but already dark outside.

This is Wales, always Wales; and my body is going into hibernation. Humans don't hibernate, the biologists tell us; but the only reason Welsh biologists don't oppose this statement is because they are hibernating and are too far sleepy to say anything at all.

But perhaps this is the solution to my dilemma!

Winter lasts for six months in Wales, so I am only truly living half a year every year. I am hibernating the rest of the time, if not in body then in soul. This means my age is exactly half of what it is. I am not fifty but only twenty-five. The shivery months added up into years don't count. They aren't properly *lived*. They are only endured. . . .

This is the defence I will use against the Queen.

A country where rain falls sideways will be full of people who learn how to keep one side of their bodies dry. This is a source of resentment to the clouds and winds, who want people to be thoroughly soaked on all sides equally. But you can't have your cake and eat it. This saying, which I've always regarded as a very daft piece of traditional wisdom, suggests that the moment you are holding a cake you won't be able to put it into your mouth. Why not? Is it monumentally dense, too heavy for mortal man to lift, or is there an electromagnetic forcefield preventing the cake from entering the gullet? But of course I am being disingenuous. I know that what this saying actually means is that:

You can't (a) have a cake, (b) eat it, (c) still have it. It's a three-stage process. The rain and wind can't blow sideways to stop Welsh people using an umbrella to protect themselves and at the same time soak those people on both sides. The rain comes horizontally at you from the front, and your front, which is absolutely drenched, shields your back from the water. This is a simple case of physics or geometry. The rain pelts the right side of your head, blown sideways by a collaborative gale; so how can it also pelt the left side? Which reminds me: the heads of most Welsh men are bald. This is because they are slowly evolving to become more waterproof. Shiny, waxy, hairless heads.

When the rain comes sideways, the misery of our one half guards the other half. This is self-sacrifice. You can't have your cake and eat it. You can, however, leave a cake out in the rain. The singer Donna Summer explained how and why this is possible, and speculated on the result, in her cover version of the epic song 'McArthur Park'. Apparently her cake took a long time to bake and the recipe, which is lost, isn't one readily available. In fact it seems to be a massively abstruse recipe and beyond any hope of recovery. A cake in the rain will shelter its own base, but this is very small consolation. As for Donna Summer, her surname is one that in Wales is regarded as a nonsense word.

> "The best thing one can do when it's raining is to let it rain."
>
> (Longfellow)

Swansea has existed in one form or another for almost a thousand years. It was founded by Vikings who rounded the headland in their longships, saw the location and said to themselves, "Not bad, a bit damp, but you can't have everything. Let's stop here."

It is pretty damn obvious that it's a city that gets a lot of rainfall. One might have hoped that over the span of an entire millennium, the people who run the city would have made efforts to accommodate the fact it is such a wet place. I mean, if you are going to build a city in the rain, the wisest course of action is surely to make certain that it is a city of arcades, covered walkways, colonnades, roofed areas, sheltered bastions, and that thoroughfares are protected by awnings.

But no such luck in Swansea! It has been planned the same way one would plan a city that doesn't get much rainfall. It is entirely exposed to the elements. Crossing busy roads means that pedestrians are going to get a double soaking, once from the rain and another from the cars that splash flooded potholes and other puddles over them. The council doesn't care. Its employees are safe and dry in their taxpayer-funded insulated offices. They are probably in league with the rain.

The characters in this work are not real characters; they are simply there so that something can happen to them. The conventional rules of fiction don't interest me much, though they must be acknowledged, and hardly any attempt has been made to apply orthodox compositional methods to this present work. There are certainly no 'characters' that a reader can identify with. Opportunities for empathy are very limited. But what's so great about ersatz empathy anyway?

A lack of empathy is considered to be the big modern sin and I often see the accusation used as a weapon, but what actually is empathy? It's the ability to put yourself in the shoes of another person and feel their suffering. In other words, it is transferred egotism. If you are empathic it suggests you can only feel sorry for someone if you can imagine that you are that person. This is rank egotism. I am more interested in compassion, which is feeling pity for someone or something without a selfish need to pretend you are that person or thing.

I once said all this to a friend of mine, a fellow called Stuart Ross, and he responded that empathy is more of an affective response to a person's emotional state, not a rational assessment of another's situation "as if I were them". The affective response to another's emotional state for an empathic person could be described as experiencing an emotional state similar to the one being observed. This did not strike him, he added, as being in line with the workings of the ego. Empathy isn't something that one chooses to have; it just happens.

In other words it is involuntary egotism, I said.

Stuart was a remarkable man and I am grateful to him for many reasons, not the least being that he was an amazing pizza chef. He cooked folded pizzas as well as the normal kind; and they were like pastry volcanoes. A prod of a fork tine and geyser steam would erupt from the crust in a most satisfying manner. His folded pizzas were really like a tastier version of the early geology of the planet. But this was a talent incidental to his love of music, which was truly profound.

He played the bass guitar in a band that did complex music with jazz undercurrents; and later formed his own band that was less abstract and more engaged with the contemporary world. I admired both his technical competence and his restless desire for innovation. His stage presence was also exemplary. Anyone who played in the Welsh music scene back then had to cope with all kinds of peculiar audience members. Venues tended to be pubs full of inebriated persons.

I don't know if those drunkards believed they were empathizing with that man up there on the little stage, but clearly they thought they were at least partly in his shoes, because they would be overcome with the urge to give him helpful advice. This advice couldn't wait for the end of the gig. It had to be delivered right there, right then, bawled and slurred as loudly as possible across the crowded pub and accompanied by flailing gestures in order to make the meaning clearer.

How sweet to be given advice on technique and style by a slobbering buffoon who is skating in his own vomit across the floor of a pub selling low quality over-priced beer! But that's what happened and probably still happens, for all I know. I avoid pubs now. I never had the talent, drive or confidence to perform music in pubs the way that Stuart did. But a few years later I was offered a chance to bang the congas and bongos in a club specializing in Latin and African dance, and because that music is more to my taste, I agreed as an experiment.

And so I experienced just a little of what Stuart had to put up with. It was much milder than his ordeal, of course, and the people who gave me advice were rarely drunk. They tended to be men, bald men usually, who wanted to be helpful, who found the urge to impart wisdom impossible to resist, who liked to put their mouths close to my ear while I was playing and tell me I was doing it all wrong, that they had learned the congas and bongos in Cuba and could do it better than me, that I should hit the drums a different way, like this, and that they had actually been to Cuba and had gone to Cuba and had spent time in Cuba.

"When I lived in Cuba . . ."

Such advice isn't real advice. It puts me in mind of a man who is walking down a road who knows that it's a long road and will take a long time to get to the end, but is determined to keep going anyway. On the side of the road there is a telephone. What is it doing out here, miles from anywhere? As the man passes it, the phone begins to ring. Curious, he goes over and answers it. A voice on the other end of the line says, "I am further down the road than you are. Yes! I wanted to tell you this. I wanted to give you a helpful tip. I am further than you."

No, this work isn't a conventional fiction with characters and plot. It's not an invitation for a reader to suspend their disbelief and become immersed in an imaginary world that will hopefully seem as real as the outer one. It is just me saying stuff about things. . . .

Any explanation of how this work came to be written should appear at the end of the text rather than being placed here, randomly amongst the other loosely connected passages. It would be more suitable as an afterword. I seem to have jumped the gun this time.

But why is it considered wrong to "jump the gun"? Surely it is better than allowing yourself to be shot or bayoneted? My shoes are fitted with springs extracted from my broken mattress and I am able to bounce high over many styles of muskets and rifles.

If only that messenger had also jumped the gun! The fable would be damaged, it's true, but the Pope would have missed his target. Before he could have reloaded, a bear that was a Catholic would have come in for confession, foiling the needless slaying.

You know how it is when you read a book that you instantly connect with on some deep level? It might be the story or the language or the dilemmas faced by the characters or simply the attitudes expressed by the prose. At last you feel you have met a kindred spirit. This author speaks directly to you in a way that not many others do.

The standard explanation for this phenomenon is that the author of the book has had similar life experiences to you. It is the experiences that are shared. Maybe the personality of the author and your personality are also parallel, which means you process those experiences in a similar manner, and the end result is a personal identification. So you are fellow travellers through life, not necessarily on a circular bus, and you support and succor each other during the grueling journey.

But could the real reason that the book speaks so profoundly to you be that you are the reincarnation of the author? In this optional explanation it is not the experiences that bond the reader to a writer, but the fact that the reader once *was* the writer. It is this one-on-one relationship that matters and not the experiences. In other words, the reader is predisposed to enjoy anything the author writes because he is reading himself. One can dislike one's own work, of course, but in this case one is reading oneself at such a distance that one thinks one is reading someone entirely different. Thus there is no shame in disliking what one is reading; and without shame one tends to relax and enjoy things properly.

I am just speculating, of course. Don't shoot the speculator!

I sometimes believe that I am the reincarnation of various authors whose books have affected me profoundly. The problem arises when the authors turn out to have still been alive after I was born. Is it possible for a living person to be reincarnated prematurely?

Wilson believes that it is. But what does he know?

Apart from lots and lots of things!

I would hate to be a reincarnation of Wilson. He is clockwork and it's unknown whether his eventual demise will count as a death in the regular way; but if it does and reincarnation happens to be true, then someone or something is going to end up with his brass soul. One day, strolling down an avenue, they will pass a bookshop.

A book in the window glimpsed out of a corner of their eye will make them retrace their steps and peer at it more carefully. *Wind Me Up Please,* a novel by Wilson. How intriguing! They will go into the shop, purchase it, take it home and read it. "This author speaks to me!" they will declare to themselves. "He had similar life experiences to me and his personality and mine are also parallel, which means I'm processing those experiences in a similar manner," they'll conclude.

Conversely there are texts we admire without feeling that the author as an individual has a correlation with us in any way. We read their books and appreciate them for what they are. Such authors are those who we are not reincarnations of. We really are fellow passengers and the bus is spherical rather than circular and called the world.

I recently read Richard Brautigan's *Trout Fishing in America* and this highly unconventional 'novel' caught my imagination more strongly than any book has done for a long time. This doesn't mean I regard it as better than other books I've read, for instance, in the past ten years, merely that I perceive it to offer a new approach to the art of writing fiction, and it is an approach that especially appeals to me because it is more suited to my abilities than most other methods I know.

I say a 'new' approach, but I don't know if it's really that. Perhaps it's simply more blatant in the way it employs metafiction, author intrusion, a frame that permits a very loose internal structure while still managing to give the appearance of an integral whole.

The novel is Brautigan just saying stuff about things. There's no real story, no true characters, no plot or even narrative development. There is randomness, chunks of whimsical self-aware 'routines' that happen to be glued by the overall conceit of a quest that ultimately is not important at all to the presentation of the material and the way it works on the mind of a reader. This quest is a malleable construct, a frame that can morph into anything else, including new characters.

Soon after reading the novel, I knew I wanted to do something along roughly similar lines myself. I wanted to write a novel that was me saying stuff about things rather than having to invent believable characters and a plot with measured incidents and resolutions. And that's what I am doing right now. Not that characters have no role at all, but they aren't the focus of the intention of the work. They are only there so that I can talk around them. Cloud Farming is my Trout Fishing.

Brautigan is a writer whose name I had been aware of for many years but whom I had never sampled. I came late to the party. Is going late to a party really bad? Most of the guests have gone home already; there's less noise, less awkwardness, less desperation.

Whether Richard Brautigan was a literary genius of the highest order or not is a moot point. He was certainly an original and refreshing voice in modern culture. I say 'was' because he is dead and has been for quite a while, alas, having shot himself presumably because of depression when his last published novel only sold fifteen thousand copies. His star had fallen since the 1960s, when he was very fashionable.

He caught the zeitgeist by accident; but then the zeitgeist moved on. It happens to the best of us. The irony for me is that if one of my books sold fifteen thousand copies I would die not of a self-inflicted gunshot but from injuries acquired from bounding around the house in utter glee on the very spring-loaded shoes that allow me to jump guns.

I have heard suicide described as "selfish" and this is something else that bewilders me. The world seems to be full of bewildering things. How can it be selfish if there's no *self* left at the end? For something to be selfish it must flatter or nurture the self as a priority, ignoring the needs of others. I fail to see how extinguishing oneself achieves this. When one is dead, the most obvious needs that are being ignored by the expired person are those helpful to themselves, for example the need to breathe and have a beating heart pumping blood around the body.

It would appear to me that suicide is a selfless act, because there is no *self* remaining when the task has been committed successfully. Maybe the critics of the process mean that unsuccessful suicide is selfish. Yes, I can see the logic in that. If one jumps off a bridge wearing petticoats that act like accidental parachutes and break one's fall into a raging river, landing one tenderly in a large canoe that happens to be rushing downstream, one can possibly be regarded as selfish. The self remains and has flattered and nurtured itself with an amazing exploit.

The owner of the canoe is none other than Boxhound Rummage, who I invented just now for the purpose of saving the person in petticoats. He has burned his bridges, which is why he is in a canoe and why a sack of crumpets waiting to be toasted is by his feet as he shoots the rapids of this river. Rapids don't always allow themselves to be shot, they can jump the gun on springs coiled from the eddies and vortices that swirl in their own margins. Yes, they have margins. They must be writers and there are few things worse than fiction about writers.

That's why Boxhound's trying to shoot them, for the good of the page and the world. And now he has a beautiful companion with him, Primella Limpet, who billows like a sleeve with an artificial heart on it, her archaic clothes settling around them like descending stormclouds. "I'm not really very selfish, you know," she says, and Boxhound nods without taking his eyes off the angry waters or his hands off his paddle for a moment. "But I get depressed sometimes, living in Wales and all, and that's why I leaped off the bridge," she adds languorously.

"That's another darned bridge I'm going to burn!" Boxhound cries in his booming baritone. "So that no one else can ever try to kill themselves by plummeting from it. I promise you!"

Primella sighs rapturously as they bob and dash.

The point about not having a self when you are dead is a subject I want to pursue further, because it has a direct bearing on something that Margaret Thatcher, a famous prime minister of Britain, once said about people who travel on buses. She said that anyone "over the age of twenty-six who still uses a bus can count themselves a failure in life."

I have thought about this quite a lot since she said it. For example, last night I watched a bus full of people pass me on the road. It was raining as always and the bus splashed people who weren't on it. But the people sitting on the bus didn't seem especially dry or happy. They had blank faces and remote eyes, minds sunk into the slurry of worry just as Atlantis sank into the seabed of a younger ocean long ago.

Most, if not all of them, were older than twenty-six.

But there was one thing common to all of them that stood out with an intensity so sharp that nothing could blunt it. They were *alive*. They may not have been particularly enjoying life, but they were alive anyway, thus still in a position to experience brilliant things one day, still in a position to be lucky sometime, still on the move.

Unlike Thatcher, who is dead. Thatcher, who no longer exists, who can't travel on any mode of transport. Who can't see, feel, touch anything at all. Who can't be happy or even miserable. Thatcher, a rotting corpse somewhere underground, who even if dug up and propped on a seat in a bus wouldn't understand anything about the journey. Once you are dead, you have no self; you are nothing at all.

That is the real failure at life, being dead. Thatcher, right now, is more of a failure than anyone on any bus anywhere. I must also point out that I am not yet over twenty-six. I have proved this thanks to my habits of hibernation. Even if Thatcher's dictum was correct, which it isn't, I still would be free to catch a bus, including Mondaugen's circular bus, with no tarnishing of my reputation, to Egypt or anywhere else.

I know what some of you are thinking. If the Queen has disguised herself as a bear once, she can do it again; so maybe the bear that was a Catholic that went to visit the Pope for confession wasn't a real bear but the Queen inside a costume. In that case, instead of saving the messenger from being shot, she wouldn't have needed to send him to the Vatican at all, because she intended to make the trip herself.

Messengers are usually employed simply as the means of conveyance of a message. But *this* messenger was a part of the message that couldn't be omitted. If the Queen had delivered the message herself, while going to confession dressed as a bear, it would no longer mean what she wanted it to mean, but would be a new message, a rewritten message, and the Holy Father's musket would have shot her.

> "Don't be angry with the rain; it simply does not know how to fall upwards."
>
> (Vladimir Nabokov)

Solutions to the problem of the endless rain in Wales have been numerous and varied but few have been implemented and none have worked. A vast umbrella covering the entire nation was attempted; but the clouds formed under the canopy, sheltering themselves from the sun that they dread and raining more heavily than before from joy. Then the umbrella blew inside out and Wales was left with a giant pole planted in its geographical centre with a few shreds of black fabric flapping near its summit. What plausible attraction does that hold for tourists?

Mondaugen was commissioned to try turning the clouds upside-down in the vague hope that an inverted cloud might discharge its rain upwards into outer space. He invented a cloud flipper and launched it one morning from his rooftop. It scoured the airspace above Wales, flipping the clouds one by one until all of them were on their backs. Much to the surprise of many of us, the clouds did indeed start raining upwards. But our gladness was short lived. It continued to rain on us too; and this rain was oilier and more horrid than the previous rainfall.

What was happening? It was quite easy to work out. The raindrops are prisms that create rainbows; this has already been explained. Now that the rain was falling upwards, these rainbows were also inverted. Instead of an arch with its feet widely planted on the ground and the apex of its elegant curve grazing the heavens, the curve now wallowed in thick mud and the legs of the rainbow stuck helplessly into the sky. An inverted rainbow is a grotesque sight, I don't know why. It is somehow degrading. These were monochrome rainbows, already dismal.

The crocks of hideous soup at the ends of the elevated legs were now also upside-down and the contents were pouring out. The mouldy juice of decayed chips and pies fell onto us in torrents. We shrieked and ran hither and thither, seeking shelter; but blinded by slime many went in the wrong direction and ended up racing across fields that were fully exposed to the glutinous downpours. I was one of these unfortunates. Then I shouted that we could find shelter under sheep! But this proved impossible. I gasped at what I saw as I wiped my vision clear.

The sheep were lying on their backs with legs in the air and they were raining upwards. Their rain was colliding with the descending rain of the crocks of soup and the splashy clash was abysmal to mortal minds. There seemed to be a competition in progress, sheep versus crocks, and nobody with any sense would dare to bet on the outcome. I won't state that it was absolutely the wettest day of my life, but it was certainly in the top five of such days. Luckily Mondaugen soon reversed the procedure by inventing a nifty machine to flip cloud flippers.

He was never asked again to tackle the issue of excess precipitation in the land of Wales. Incidentally, the Welsh name for soup is *cawl* and the particular form of soup that fell from those inverted rainbows was so foul and diabolic that scholars believe it to be the sweat of a monster; and not just any old monster but the interstellar octopus entity known as Cthulhu, who was invented by the writer H.P. Lovecraft. This seems plausible. The cawl of Cthulhu is a meal unfit for sane men. It is seasoned with nihilism and served with the croutons of doom.

To the Lovecraftian pessimist, the half-empty glass is always full with the sweat of interstellar octopus entities.

While we are talking about morbid and frightful things, I should declare that the antiques dealer Fiddly Buttons turned out to be as sinister as you have probably already concluded he would be, with a name like that. His clothes consisted entirely of overlapping buttons of different sizes, so that one assumed he was actually a creature made of eyes rather than a human being. He was, in essence, a Gothic feller; and when he paid me a visit, I rather regretted engaging him for the task of judging the value of my attic clouds. By then it was already too late.

"I trust I'm the first to inspect them?" he asked.

"Indeed you are," I replied.

"That's good, very good indeed, because I don't want anyone to cheat you. I have a rival in this business, you see, and he is a rascal. I wouldn't want you getting involved with him."

"You are the first."

He rubbed his hands together in a melodramatic fashion and twirled the waxed ends of his dastardly moustaches.

Moustaches are waxed in Wales not primarily for the sake of fashion but in a futile attempt to waterproof them from the rain. There is a saying that was coined by

Wilson but is pertinent anyway: the waterproof of the pudding is in the waxing. The reason why Wilson coins sayings is so that he can spend those coins in shops.

It remains to be determined what a clockwork man can find to spend a coin on. Maybe he doesn't care about that; the act of spending is enough. The ways of Wilson are not our ways. But let's return to Fiddly Buttons. I wanted to get him out of my house as quickly as possible. We were in the attic. He was systematically tickling the bellies of my clouds and making clicking noises with a pale tongue.

The tongue wasn't his. He had drawn it from a bag when he began his valuation of my accumulated cumulus. I mean that it *was* his, but didn't belong to his mouth. Clearly it was one of the tools of his trade, but my doubts about the man were increasing every moment. Yet I knew him to be a furniture expert with a reputation for reliability. Something felt amiss and I couldn't put my finger on it. . . .

Which reminds me of the time I met Cloudier Sheepier, the archetypal Welsh beauty, a rain-drenched goddess who commanded enormous sums to model clothes, perfumes and long green onions. I was overawed by the stylish gorgeousness of Cloudier, but there was something not quite right and I couldn't put my finger on it, partly because she wouldn't let me, she wasn't that sort of girl, and partly because the something that wasn't right was cryptic and arcane and ineffable.

Later I learned that Cloudier Sheepier didn't physically exist but was only a form of communal hallucination generated by the heavy raindrops that pelt the exposed skulls of Welsh men. For some reason women were immune to that particular mirage. Could it be that women wear hats more often than men nowadays? Certainly!

Anyway, I hope to get Fiddly Buttons out of the way, because I don't actually want too many characters in this text. The point of this text isn't to be an audition for characters. There are only two real characters in this story: the reader and author. The text is the playground between them. I don't know how Fiddly ended up having more than just one paragraph to himself. So let's terminate his career.

"Something funny about this one," he remarked.

"What do you mean?" I said.

"This cloud. It has a distended tummy. Never felt anything like it and I am wondering if it's serious?"

"Might it be pregnant with lightning bolts?"

"But it's not a thundercloud. It's a light fluffy white cloud. Let me just prod it with this hatpin that I keep behind my ear for emergencies. It's an excellent example of the pin-maker's art, solid silver and engraved along its entire length with scenes of hats from antiquity, including the headgear of Socrates and Caesar. Watch now!"

And he jabbed the cloud with the hatpin. There was a loud bang and a big lightning bolt struck him in the middle of the chest. It was yellow and really shaped like a zigzag. He didn't scream, he didn't have time for that, but merely exhaled his breath, which now smelled of ozone. Then he was reduced to cinders and his clothes fell apart. Buttons rolled about my feet or span away into dark attic corners.

"Sir, you are undone!"

But he didn't reply to my malign quip.

That's one option. Another possibility is that when the cloud ruptured it revealed the hidden occupant who had been lurking inside a long time, waiting for his opportunity. None other than the sworn enemy of Fiddly Buttons, the rival furniture dealer he had described as a rascal, Doodah Zips, who wore clothes made entirely from conjoined zips of different lengths, so that one felt he was a creature formed of grins rather than a human being. He was, in essence, a second Gothic feller, one to oppose and grimly cancel out the first.

The terrible and epic fight between them resulted in mutually assured destruction, a little pile of buttons mixed with zips and no shred of flesh to bulk it out into a sensible shape. These buttons and zips, with the aid of a broom, can now be swept through the open trapdoor and collected in a zinc bucket positioned beneath. This bucket will then be emptied into the gutter, where the rainwater should sweep the detritus towards the sea, and two superfluous characters will be removed with little trouble. However, I won't get money for my clouds.

Unless you are interested in buying them?

Creatures made of eyes or grins are monsters; and Wales is home to many monsters already. When we read books or watch films in which monsters feature we might be afraid of them, but rational thought should lead us to the conclusion they are generally less harmful than the humans they meet. More often than not, the humans beat the monsters; and surely we act in a most illogical manner when we recoil from a werewolf, vampire or robot gorilla, but say hello to a person we just happen to meet on the street who we have never even seen before.

This person is statistically more vicious. I have read and viewed with my own eyes books and films in which ordinary men slaughter the worst avatars of evil, men like the person we said "good morning, nice day" to, while tipping our hats, if we had hats on and it wasn't raining too heavily, as if there was no peril in greeting him at all. And yet men like him drive stakes through vampire hearts, shoot poor werewolves with silver bullets and unplug robot gorillas in uncountable horror climaxes! Indeed it's true that humans are the real monsters.

The most absurd fear is the fear of the living skeleton. The instant we see such a skeleton, we run away. We're scared of skeletons, but we have one inside us; so how can we run away from them? The skeleton comes with us as we flee and goes wherever we go. The skeleton inside us enables us to run away in the first place. How can anything escape from itself? Even if we entered a maze we wouldn't be able to shake off the skeleton. Being a human who is afraid of skeletons is no less foolish than being a piecrust frightened of its own tasty filling. . . .

This discussion about skeletons reminds me of a girl who confessed that she wanted to "jump my bones" and I agreed. So she killed me, boiled off my flesh, extracted my skeleton, selected the most suitable bones such as my femurs, propped these on stands, and used them as hurdles. After long months of intense practice she broke the Welsh record for the one hundred metres distance in that event, but it goes without saying I wasn't able to applaud her achievement because I was dead.

The fish and other sea creatures that swim along the streets of Wales are in short supply today. I wonder if someone has been overfishing them? I wouldn't be surprised. Soon there will be a severe shortage of walruses in our public spaces and what will we do then? We'll have to purchase them from the Wal Я Us store at exorbitant rates. I hate going there. The items on display are plasticky and their tusks are poorly designed. I note that a recently netted walrus that was swimming through the grounds of Cardiff Castle turned out to be one of Mondaugen's land subs and its occupant an envoy of the Pope. The fisherman who caught him threw him back rather than deep-frying him for supper, I think.

I often wonder why women evolved to cry a lot. I think maybe that it was prehistorically in order to attract thirsty lions and tigers and thus give men more opportunities to be heroic and defend their mates; and also to have a chance of sleeping with two blankets.

When two different things are put together, they don't always fight, like a tiger and lion blanket. Sometimes they combine their resources and create something worthwhile. For instance, when Rudyard Kipling encountered Dr Moreau on Skull Island and ended up writing the story 'The Man Who Would be Kong' there was no trouble.

Dr Oxygen and Mr Hydrogen (a dialogue)

Hydrogen: Hello, how do you do?
Oxygen: Pleased to meet you. Do you come here often?
Hydrogen: I'm just passing through.
Oxygen: Me too. I decided to go for a little aimless drifting about in the lower atmosphere and found myself straying into the airspace above this funny little country.
Hydrogen: Well, I'm heading in the other direction so I'll just bid you farewell and wish you good luck.
Oxygen: Thanks! The same to you.
Hydrogen: If you could let go of me please. . .
Oxygen: What do you mean? It is *you* who are holding onto to *me*.
Hydrogen: That's a lie. You have me in an embrace.
Oxygen: I beg your pardon? How dare you accuse me of the very action that you are guilty of! Outrageous!
Hydrogen: If you don't let me go immediately I will call the police and have you arrested for assault.
Oxygen: What police? We are chemical elements.
Hydrogen: Good point. Nonetheless . . .
Oxygen: My nucleus and electrons seem to have become entangled with your nucleus and electrons. I say 'elec-

trons' but I perceive that you only have one. Would you mind disengaging it? Then I can go on my way and you can go on yours.

HYDROGEN: I am trying but our protons are snagged.

OXYGEN: Just pull harder, will you?

HYDROGEN: I did but it has made everything worse!

OXYGEN: What's happening? We seem to be slowly combining into one substance with unique properties. Oh, this is horrid! I feel I am losing my individual identity. Unhand me!

HYDROGEN: My vision has blurred. I am melting. Help!

WATER: Ha ha! Now I am stronger than before! I will punish those stupid mortals below by falling on their heads again and again and again. I'll pay them back for daring to exist on the ground! Rain shall be the fate of that funny little country until the end of time. Its denizens will rue the day that oxygen and hydrogen met in their sky! I am water and no mercy will ever be shown by me!

Hell is a basement flat with endless rooms, all mouldy, connected by dim and depressing corridors, also mouldy. Many of the lightbulbs don't work and have never worked; and those that do are of a very low wattage. The carpets are worn and filthy, the windows are grimy and nothing can ever be seen through them, the wallpaper is bubbling and peeling. This is Hell for Welsh people; the hells intended for people of other lands are possibly quite different. Sometimes a torrent of diabolical rainwater washes along these corridors and carries away any soul caught in it to distant regions of the infinite flat that are nearly identical.

Just because the interior of this flat is covered with a ceiling doesn't mean it doesn't rain indoors. The clouds drift up and down the corridors just the same as the damned souls do. This is a Welsh Hell for sure. There are rooms full of nothing but damp coal; others bulging with rotten chips, pies green with decay, beer that tastes of socks. Occasionally a room may be bearable for a few hours or even days, but always something will come along to spoil the reprieve. Beds will suddenly explode like bombs, their mattress springs scattering like spores.

A few walls are adorned with framed pictures of grim scenes in other parts of the flat or photographs of dead sheep in the rain. There is also the occasional badly painted mural. These murals depict the same few themes over and over again. Muddy puddles reflecting dismal skies, drowned pit ponies, rotting schoolchildren, evicted tenants squatting in the rain, junkie muggers beating old women, hunched people shambling along in queues that are closed circles, cars deliberately driving through flooded potholes and splashing pedestrians on pavements.

One of the most common of these murals is a large blurred face of the chubby alcoholic coward Dylan Thomas. There's going to be an upsurge of ire against me for describing him that way. I know this. Bear with me, as the Pope said when he took a shit in the woods, adding, "and then I'll hear your confession." "Sure, take your time", replied the bear who was a Catholic. But let us not stray too far from the point! The mural is blurred because the artist lacked talent, but also because the subject himself lived in a haze, his face an inebriated smudge.

For those who haven't heard of him, Dylan is the most famous Welsh writer of all; and Wales is enormously proud of him. He wrote poetry and prose, the bulk of his work being completed in his youth, and he sat down even more and drank a lot of beer and whisky. He was chubby because he had an unhealthy lifestyle; he was an alcoholic because he had a physical and a mental dependency on alcohol; he was a coward because he feigned illness to avoid fighting the Nazis in World War II. These are simple facts as well as value judgments. Yes they are.

Now we might agree, you and I, that to scorn a man for being chubby is unreasonable; that to despise a man for alcoholism is uncharitable; that to mock a man for fearing death or mutilation is unrealistic. The failings of Dylan Thomas are human and not out of the ordinary. Furthermore we must remember that obesity, intoxicant dependency and timidity all have genetic, environmental and circumstantial factors; in short, that his chubby alcoholic cowardice was not his fault but just the way things panned out and the same could happen to any of us.

This is all true. But if there is no shame in being chubby, alcoholic or cowardly, if these weaknesses are accidents of time and place of birth, of biology and background, why did you bristle when I described him thus? If he should not be blamed for being a chubby alcoholic coward, why do you oppose this definition? Clearly on some level you *do* regard chubby alcoholic cowardice as undesirable. The choice of my words and tone is the problem. I guess I could have announced him to be a cuddly drunken pacifist and everything would be all right.

But I can equally argue that my aggressiveness in this matter isn't my fault, that it has genetic, environmental and circumstantial factors, that I should be allowed to speak as I please and that criticism of my selection of words is as unfair as my treatment of Dylan's character. Well, we can play this game all day. Perhaps you have a fondness for Dylan Thomas, for his work; you have decided to make allowances for him, allowances you won't make for me. I am old enough to know that the world doesn't work in any other way. So please continue.

But I have the opposite of a fondness for him. You are biased towards Dylan; I am biased against. Both biases are irrational, arbitrary, let's not be deluded about this; our difference of opinion on the issue has nothing to do with justice and everything to do with sentiment. I have suffered an overload of Dylan in my life in Wales, too much exposure to his cult has eroded my tolerance and given me a reflexive distaste for anything to do with him; and yes, it's unfair, but it's also human and natural, as human and natural as chubby alcoholic cowardice.

In Wales, especially in Swansea, one can be forgiven for thinking that Wales has never had a writer other than Dylan. The council utilises him at every opportunity, however inappropriate the situation or occasion. They milk his chins and jowls without surcease; and the milk that dribbles from his posthumous reputation is rancid with foamy beer and distilled spirits. Dylan this, Dylan that. And yes, he was a good writer; and no, I have no hatred for his work. But his cult makes me nauseous and I fight back by seeking out weak spots and trying to strike.

It is a futile exercise, I know. Calling him a chubby alcoholic coward is more likely to reflect poorly on me than on him. That's the way of the modern world. Nor do I presume I am safe from chubbiness, alcoholism or cowardice; I want to believe I have none of those weaknesses but can only be absolutely confident that one is utterly alien to my nature. Don't mistake me for a smug chap. I may be many things you don't like, but I am fully aware that almost anything can happen to anyone. Ivor the Beak flies high but only until his wings rot away.

My own candidate for best Welsh writer ever is Arthur Machen, who had a much wider thematic range than Dylan, a deeper understanding of the fact that life is essentially a mystery, a restless curiosity about finding methods of throwing aside the veils of illusion that we continually drape ourselves with, a fervent desire to work with ideas. In contrast, Dylan was little more than a descriptive writer with a melodious way of commenting on things that don't especially interest me. But this is all just my opinion, a question of taste, and not the taste of beer.

Anyway . . . to return to the basement flat that is Hell for the Welsh, I should add that the murals sometimes detach themselves from the walls and float down the corridors, following rain or preceding it, the blurred face of Dylan opening and closing its mouth as it attempts to swallow the clouds in the hope they are the foamy heads of beers. Any souls in those corridors at the time will be gulped down too and excreted from the back of his head much later. He doesn't care. Fiddly Buttons has just arrived in Hell together with his nemesis Doodah Zips.

They clutch each other for comfort, then push each other away, drawn and repelled in equal measure. Suddenly at the end of a warped corridor that turns a sharp right angle like a snapped arm, comes a head around the corner. It is a drifting mural of Dylan and these new arrivals are unlucky enough to encounter it during their first minutes of damnation. Fiddly and Doodah shriek and run, but they trip over each other and nearer looms the drunkard's gaping mouth as they sprawl and try to get up. Mushrooms on the carpet snap off under their frantic fingers.

The paint of the mural has run in the rain. Dylan's curly hair is now so smeared that it resembles the helmet of a knight. How ironic! "Do not go gentle into that knight!" Fiddly and Doodah warn each other. Maybe now they are in Hell they will become friends; the truth is that they always had a love-hate relationship. The Welsh Hell is an appalling place. Every hundred years the landlord calls around to pick up the rent from every cursed soul trapped there. But less about that! Wilson once wrote a poem that is a sort of parody of Dylan's work. I will search for it.

Oh yes, the face swallowed Fiddly and Doodah; then licked its lips. It continued to drift along the corridor, turning corners and entering rooms, coming back out, retracing its route, getting lost, finally attaching itself to a wall in some other part of the labyrinth. National Poetry Day is coming up soon. I will try to find Wilson's poem before that. I know I said I was dead after that girl jumped my bones, but I was only jesting. I am capable of finding the poem without too many difficulties. A dead person couldn't really do that. She didn't jump my bones at all.

She jumped Wilson's bones instead. His bones are made of brass and are denser and heavier than mine. When she failed to jump high enough over the hurdles, her shins knocked against them and she injured herself and had to retire from athletics. I put the bones back inside Wilson and he thanked me with a polite nod. In fact, if I am going to be really honest, I *was* murdered by that woman but only temporarily. I wanted to visit Hell to see if the special oboe tune could be found down there. Wilson brought me back from the dead by replacing my bones.

We do favours for each other all the time. This is the best way to live, in Wales or anywhere else for that matter, and I trusted him to resurrect me after I went to Hell on my musical quest. The girl, by the way, was none other than Primella Limpet, because it's more efficient to reuse her than invent another character at this juncture. This was before she jumped off the bridge. She likes jumping things and from things, it's as simple as that. Jumping, skipping; all those kinds of activities. She would skip this sentence if she were reading it now, for instance.

In Noah's era it rained for forty days and forty nights without pause. That is what the Bible claims, anyway. When I was at school and our teacher told us this in class, we all gasped together, an immense communal gasp from the gathered pupils that was like the yawning of the biggest giant in any legend anywhere. Forty days and forty nights! "So dry!" we gasped in astonished envy. "So dry! Lucky Noah! To dwell in a place where rain falls for only forty days and forty nights!"

It seemed a ludicrously short amount of time for rain to fall. In Wales this story has the opposite effect from the one intended. It isn't cautionary but encouraging. Noah's contemporaries sinned and as a result it rained for forty days and forty nights; then the rain stopped. The conclusion we drew was that sinning was good, that sin would give us dryness. But we didn't know how to sin back then, we lacked the skills and equipment, so in the end the tale of Noah didn't help us.

A Welsh version of the famous fable would have to take into account the special conditions that exist in this country. All the details should be reversed. Instead of a wooden ark built to float on water and stuffed with animals, a Welsh Noah must construct a watery vessel designed to stand on dryness and stuffed with vegetables.

It stops raining for forty days and forty nights. This new ark is a vast chunk of ice, a man-made glacier that contains within it frozen peas, beans, leeks.

The name of the man who created it is Haon, a reversal of Noah. His surname is Why. He is Haon Why; which, if you care to check, you will find is a real town in Wales as well as a joke and a question. The dryness stops and the rains resume and Haon releases the opposites of a raven and a dove, in other words an eel and a cod, to find wet ground. At last his ice ark comes to rest in deep lake known as Tarara and an inverted rainbow appears in the heavens as a divine promise.

Other Bible incidents can be similarly reversed in order to be applied to Wales. A fish that swallows a man becomes a man who spits out a fish, one of the fish that swim through the air; the man's mouth was open and it swam in by mistake. Or the Last Supper, which when reversed becomes the First Breakfast and features people tucking in to chips and pies at an ungodly hour. The Last Supper table was straight, so the Welsh one must be round, like the ring-mark of a beer glass.

Let me reiterate the conceit that forms the frame for the disparate routines and passages of this work, namely that a flock of clouds are being dipped in your consciousness one by one. The longer fragments and outtakes are grown clouds; the shorter ones are cloudlets. So I am not the writer of the text; Wilson is a writer, yes, but he's not the writer of this work. Nobody wrote this work, the chunks of text are merely the bodies of clouds. I am just a character. I was in danger of forgetting the framing device that was supposed to bind together all the disparity, which is why I am writing this now. But I'm not actually writing it, of course. It is the body of a dipped cloud, probably a cloudlet considering its length, a cumulus lamb. If you can smell mint sauce now, you are mean.

Boxhound Rummage and Primella Limpet planned to re-enter the prose at this point, I don't know what for, but they missed the tributary turning on the raging river and were carried past by a current too powerful to paddle against, so they must continue to a destination unknown. That's perfectly fine by me. They are canoodling in the bottom of the canoe, which is why they missed the turning. Canoes are good for canoodlers.

They are sure to fall in love and get married. It's just that the honeymoon is going to come first! Like eating dessert before the main.

Exaggerations are more often true in Wales than in any other nation in the world. Last year, according to the Office of National Statistics, there were exactly 1000000000000066600000000000001 exaggerations in Wales, of which 98.7% turned out to be true. This is a curious total because it is the same as the spookiest number in existence, Belphegor's Prime, which is a palindromic prime number and also contains the digits 666 surrounded on both sides by two strings of thirteen zeros.

Honeymoons are pleasant enough. But marriage isn't always great. Let's be aware of potential disadvantages. Hitler survived several assassination attempts. Then he got married and thirty-seven hours later was dead. Coincidence? Maybe but maybe not. Wilson's story 'The Catcher in the Reich' alludes to this. Which reminds me. One Nazi plan was for a bomber aeroplane to be disguised as a cloud. Flocks of such clouds were going to be unleashed against cities and the civilians living in them; but this was one 'vengeance weapon' that never left the drawing board.

Wilson left the drawing board; he walked right off it. Mondaugen hardly ever designs his inventions on paper. He usually just tinkers with parts in a random manner until something emerges that works. With clockwork men and other artificial people he makes a special effort. Although it is correct to describe Wilson as a clockwork man, in fact the power for his brain and limbs comes from a miniature nuclear reactor inside his chest. The clockwork part of him simply controls the failsafe mechanisms that prevent the reactor from overheating. This is why Wilson must be wound up regularly; otherwise he'll go into meltdown and burn his way through the planetary crust and disappear forever.

Most people when they sit at home and write have clean hands and when they work on a farm their hands are dirty. With Wilson it's the other way around because he farms clouds and the rains wash his hands continually, but when he was a writer he often didn't bother to wash his hands before starting to type his day's quota of words.

An avid reader of James Joyce once approached the master and asked if he might "kiss the hand that wrote *Ulysses*" and Joyce replied, "No, it did a lot of other things too." And this makes me wonder about whether there is any difference between books written with clean hands and those written with dirty hands. I think there is.

Books written with dirty hands will contain germs in the gaps between the words, in the spaces between the ending of one sentence and the start of the next. The more successful the author, the more copies of the book will be printed, and the more germs spread among the reading public. The bestseller is a likely source of epidemics.

Never shake a librarian's hand! This is wise advice.

When a librarian extends a hand for you to shake it, make a motion as if you are going to grip it, but at the last instant lift your hand to your face with the thumb against your nose and wiggle your fingers. This will help to ward off bacteria, the evil eye, and fines for non-returned books. Blow a raspberry to make the gesture supreme.

Since I made that remark I have been followed everywhere by a massive hand. A paranormal hand with bibliophile's fingers. Upstairs, downstairs, down the street, through the park, it's always there when I look, a really enormous hand. I just can't shake it.

Sometimes I open a worn suitcase in an alcove in my spare room and take out copies of old magazines in which Wilson had stories published. They are falling apart now, those magazines, so I turn the pages carefully. The ink has also started to fade. His stories, although printed and distributed, are starting to unwrite themselves, the same way an Italian in a café who is eating spaghetti makes it less and less probable, as the meal proceeds, that he or anyone else is going to write a letter to his girlfriend or wife or even another man's wife with his food.

Wilson's stories are generally much more plausible than his real life. For example, here's one that is a reversal of Tarzan of the Apes. A baby male ape is shipwrecked in Wales and brought up by aristocrats; when he returns to the jungle he is able to drink cups of tea, play card games, wear cravats and be sarcastic in a way that gives him dominance over the other apes. The title of this story is 'Nazrat del Sepa', which is fitting not only because it is a reversal of the original title but because in Spanish 'sepa' means 'know' and Nazrat has knowledge.

He can wind up a gramophone in less than ten seconds and even play croquet on the lawn with a snide smile. The other apes are astonished and envious. Another thing he does is write stories on a typewriter there in the jungle, stories about a brief time in the life of Conan the Barbarian when he liked to wear makeup. This youthful phase in his intrepid career isn't well known, so Nazrat had plenty of latitude for his imagination. Sample titles include 'Eye Shadows in Zamboula', 'Red Finger Nails', 'People of the Black Eyeliner', 'Rouge in the House'.

The apes watched and decided to mimic Nazrat. Somehow they seized typewriters, lots of them, probably by raiding towns on the coast, and set to work banging the keys. There were a plentitude of apes engaged in this work. The craze caught on. Eventually not only every ape that existed but all the apes that didn't exist were busy typing. It took ten years before the news was reported back to humanity. An infinite number of apes banging typewriter keys had recreated the complete works of Francis Bacon! This bulletin was censored for the sake of culture.

The Italian in the café finished his meal and went outside. I happened to be in Italy at the time, with my oboe, seeking the tune of tunes. I had a copy of one of Wilson's books with me. "It's a classic up there with the greats," the man told me in English. I was surprised to hear this. Wilson wasn't *that* good. We were standing in a vineyard at the time. Only after he walked away did I realise I had misheard him. "A classic up there with the grapes," was what he'd actually said. I looked up and saw a battered copy of *Ulysses* entangled by the vines.

The book of Wilson's I had been reading was called *Elixirs of Youth* and it tells the story of a man who is growing old. He is not very old but he is old enough; he has recently celebrated his fiftieth birthday and he is suffused with acute nostalgia for his lost youth. His friends tell him that it isn't lost yet, that he's still relatively young, but he doesn't find such well-meaning words convincing. He remembers a legend about an alchemist living in an exotic city who created an elixir of youth.

Might this legend be based on truth? Could the alchemist still be alive and willing to share some of the elixir? The man decides to take a chance and find out for himself. The name of the exotic city is Veracity. It's not easy to find because it doesn't appear on any map, and even though a few people he asks have heard of it, they don't know in which direction it lies. But after almost one year of searching he finally stumbles into it, wanders the streets and calls out for the alchemist.

An extremely pretty girl accosts him near the market. "What is it that you desire, stranger?" she asks, and he answers that he wants a sip of the elixir of youth. "Come with me," she says; and she leads him down thin alleyways and through the doorway of a house into a room in which sits an incredibly old and gnarled hag. The room is shadowy and a small fire splutters under an iron cauldron of some bubbling liquid. The hag blinks at the newcomer. "You've come for this?"

She nods at the cauldron and the man licks his lips. "Is that really the elixir of youth, and if I drink some will I become a young man again?" It is almost too much to hope for. The hag confirms that it is the elixir and will rejuvenate him. "But there is a price to be paid," she adds. The man has been expecting this. "You may have my birthday presents, every one, in exchange," he says, "and I was given some really nice stuff." The hag laughs at him and her laughter is a cackle.

"No, the price was set long ago," she explains, "and I'll tell you what it is. The man who drinks the elixir of youth must agree to marry without prevarication the daughter of the keeper of the elixir." And at these words the man is beside himself with joy. He glances at the extremely pretty girl who accosted him and cries, "I will pay that price willingly!" He is happy beyond measure that not only is he going to be made young yet again but will acquire a lovely wife into the bargain.

The deal is made and he takes the spoon offered by the hag and dips it into the cauldron. Raising it to his lips, he sips the life-giving fluid. All at once he feels an amazing restoration of his physical powers. Strength and health flow along his veins. He flexes his limbs, enjoying the sensation of renewed vitality; then he turns to the pretty girl and offers his hand with a gentle smile. "Come here, my bride to be."

The girl frowns. She informs him that he has made a mistake, that his future wife is the decrepit hag sitting on the stool; that she, the young girl, is the alchemist who invented and imbibed the potion, thus preserving her youth, while the hag is her own daughter, who is allergic to the brew and was never able to keep it down and thus has aged normally and is soon to celebrate her eighty-seventh birthday. "She is the one you will marry and sleep with, not me," explains the pretty girl.

The man is horror-struck. But then he realises that modern readers may consider his attitude geriatrophobic, so he sighs and accepts the situation and forces a smile; and when the hag stands up to solicit a loving embrace from him, he does his best to hug her bag of clicking bones in a way that is not too obviously a grotesque parody of affection. "No need for delays, I think the wedding should take place today," says the young girl, and the hag dribbles with glee on hearing her words.

The man mutters something and the pretty girl adds, "If you refuse to consummate the marriage, the elixir you've drunk will not only wear off but turn to poison and you will die racked by agony. But let's not talk of unpleasant things! Today is a most happy occasion! You are going to be my son-in-law from now on. My name is Vera, by the way, and this city was named after me. What is your name?"

The novel ends before the man gives his name, but I am wondering if Wilson based the character on me as a sort of joke. As for myself, the real me I mean, my own quest wouldn't be for the elixir of youth but the elixir of dryness. I would search for it among the remotest hill of Wales, where I would eventually find it but not in the form I imagined. It wouldn't be a fluid in a pot but an umbrella embedded in a boulder and only the chosen one would be able to draw it out and open it.

The remotest hill of Wales can only be found by one method. First the seeker must climb to the top of the remotest hill known to him personally and then stand on tiptoe and scan the horizon for a hill even remoter, and so on, repeating the process until finally no remoter hill is seen anywhere. When this happens, it means the remotest hill has been located and in fact is the one beneath you at that very moment.

The bus full of my reflections is passing through Lebanon. I have a liking for Lebanese food. Which reminds me: I find it odd when women say to their husbands, "Why go out for burgers when you can stay at home and eat steak every night?" For one thing, it's not good to stay in the house all the time. Also if you eat steak every day you are going to suffer coronary and digestion problems. Plus the expense of eating steak on a daily basis is prohibitive for most. I am a vegetarian and prefer to go out for an Indian or Lebanese. My reflections agree with me.

The world is a hot water bottle but containing magma instead of water. I realised this last night when I was cold in bed and had to get up. My hot water bottle had gone cold. The bigger the hot water bottle, the longer it takes to cool. The Earth is so large that it's still hot after billions of years, but one day it too will go cold. And then whatever unimaginable cosmic entity it is keeping warm will get out of bed.

Cthulhu is surely that unimaginable cosmic entity; but if that's truly the case then something has gone wrong somewhere, because I can imagine him, which makes a mockery of the unimaginable part. I imagine Cthulhu as looking like a cross between the Queen and the Pope but with hundreds of tentacles tied in knots that are really tricky to undo and one very long leg with a really big foot on the end of it that is encased in a horrible old boot. I'm not saying this is how Cthulhu is, merely it's the way I imagine him, which is a totally different thing.

Most people imagine him as half octopus, half dragon. Well, that's their prerogative. I don't suppose they have seen him for real either. We are free to imagine him in any way we please; or more to the point, in any way you don't please. I intend to imagine him as a fruit. An interstellar papaya. Radio telescopes mistake him for an asteroid. If he entered our atmosphere and struck the ground the SPLAT would be extraordinary. It would be the greatest splat in creation!

A papaya died and was buried in a pawpaw's grave. . . .

Sunflowers in Wales have little clouds over them but rationalists will say they are dandelion seeds drifting through the air. But then the seeds start raining and down below is a mouse holding a cocktail umbrella. They are real clouds after all. Nothing connected with the sun will ever be allowed to remain uncovered here. That's the law.

The fat man on the bus earlier has been nameless all this time and I might leave myself open to accusations of wanting to dehumanize him if I allow him to continue much longer without a proper identity. Everybody in the world deserves respect, and though he's not really in the world because I made him up for this story, this story does exist in the world. Therefore I am going to hold back no longer and I am going to give him a name and a few personality traits he can keep forever.

His name is Meeky Chunky and as his name would suggest he is both modest and mischievous at the same time.

Continuing the theme of obesity, it's a shame that on the human body the positions of the chest and stomach aren't reversed. If they were, it would be easier to lose weight from the belly and gain musculature on the torso due entirely to the simple action of gravity.

You know those people who get increasingly intolerant as they get older? Every year I despise them more and more. . . .

I was attempting to shelter from the rain under a sunflower one morning when I was astonished to see a moonflower pass in front of it. This was the first time I have ever seen a total floral eclipse and I felt privileged to be a witness to such an extremely rare event.

I promised to share Wilson's poem that is a Dylan Thomas parody. I did look for it but I couldn't find it. And now National Poetry Day is here, so I guess I ought to write a poem myself as a substitute. I know it won't be as good at Wilson's and for that I apologise.

Today is National Poetry Day
and I agreed to write a poem for it
    just for fun
But I can't think what to say

        There are no ideas in my head
        so I think I'll just refuse
            and drink some booze instead

On second thought, I don't have any
    in the house
So I'll just play backgammon
    against a mouse

            Hey, the mouse won!

A Short List of the Principal Books of Wilson

Gremlins of the Kremlin
The Gross Prophet
Bronze Limbs Get Real
Big Hand for Waldo
Parrots of the Carob Bean
My Hags-to-Bitches Story
Precipitation Jubilation
Gnome is Where the Heart is
Lord of the Open Flies
The Lock of Love
Crystal Glooms of the Fish City
Pears Are Always Alone
The Man as Fit as a Tax Fiddle
Robot Ape Unplugged

This bibliography is far from complete, of course, because I might change my mind later about what books he has or hasn't written. I can do this as I please. The list features novels only.

No reference is made here to any of his collections of short stories or essays; nor is the present cloud farming work set in Wales considered to be, strictly speaking, one of his efforts.

But from a brief perusal of the titles we may see that he attempted the composition of novels in different genres, including grotesque espionage, religious-fiscal thriller, tropical industrial romance, science friction, wild historical chocolate-substitute adventure, snide morality tale, rain fetish, bottom of the garden phantasy, atavistic castaway frolic, bubble popping romp, fruit solitude, health and gorilla.

He was nothing if not versatile, that clockwork man!

When I am reading a book, I consult my index finger to find out the page numbers of my other fingers. My fingers often end up being inserted in a book because I tend to do this instead of using multiple bookmarks when I am reading a volume for research purposes. I leave out my index finger and keep it extended straight like the little finger of a hand holding a cup of tea, so I can easily consult it to know exactly what pages in the book my other fingers are marking. That's why it is called an index finger. This is a good tip for you too. A fingertip.

When I was much younger I was in the habit of going with my friends at night to a house we picked at random. We would lurk outside and make animal noises until the resident of the house was finally disturbed enough to come out and see what was going on.

Some of us were excellent mimics and the cacophony of sound was a rather adroit as well as truly terrific and vastly irritating impingement on the tranquility of the nocturnal hours. Sometimes we would play this trick until dawn, alarming many households.

Then I grew older and stopped making animal noises. Some skills are retained forever, such as the art of riding a bicycle; others are rapidly lost, such as the performing of long division in your head. I am not sure where pretending to be a wolf, donkey, chicken, toad, puma, phoenix, aardvark, jellyfish, squelcher, ballyhoo, etc., lies on this spectrum but I suspect I'm unable to replicate any of them with the same alacrity and verisimilitude that I once did. One of the losses of life.

I had almost forgotten about these escapades until last night when my sleep was disturbed by sounds outside my bedroom window. I could hear the voices of what was evidently a group of people in earnest dispute with each other. They were having heated discussions on numerous topics that included the correct way of swinging a croquet mallet, the proper method of elevating the little finger when clutching a cup of tea, the true author of the plays of Shakespeare, whether the Pope did really shit in the woods or not, the optimum dimensions of a canoe.

I endured this racket for at least an hour before my patience snapped. I grumbled myself out of bed, went to the window, flung it open and called down at them to shut up or move on! But at that very moment, the moon peeped from behind a passing raincloud and in the illumination it offered I saw that next to my abode was gathered a collection of animals engaged in making typical human noises for a jest. They were superb mimics too. The moment they saw my astonished face, they burst into a happy medley of roars, yelps, shrieks, grunts and yowls that expressed utter bestial mirth and loped, pranced, hopped, flapped, slithered away to safety, or else to harass some other random householder. . . .

It would have been best for me to laugh quietly and shake my head at the symmetry of it, but I was slightly troubled. They were all the animals depicted on the wall of Cardiff Castle I mentioned earlier. Had the statues come to life and left their fixtures to embark on this escapade? If so, what magic had enabled this to happen? I went back to bed and soon the rains resumed and diluted the lingering echoes of that unholy ruckus, that fake debate about human interests and etiquette.

I went on an archaeological dig and made an exciting discovery: a full set of archaeology tools from the previous decade!

That happened in the depths of one of the many forests of Wales. While I was returning from the dig I happened to meet Bigfoot coming the other way. He was on stilts and on the base of each stilt was a human shoe. He told me that he had been faking human trails for years. What a hoaxer! I congratulated him on his sense of humour.

He looked smaller than he was because his stilts were so high. In fact he hardly looked bigger or more intimidating than a very large gorilla. This made me think about Meeky Chunky and the other fat people of Wales. It occurred to me that size is really only a matter of perspective. If you think you are too large, simply stand further away and you will look smaller. If you think you are too thin, stand closer and you will look bigger. In terms of geometry, size is all about distance.

I gave him the archaeology tools I'd dug up. I had to give him something or he might have twisted my head off. He accepted them and then strode away into the darkest woodland depths.

Most archaeologists only ever find broken pots in the ruins of buildings. There must have been a hell of a lot of domestic arguments in the distant past to create so many broken pots.

Looking in the bathroom mirror I notice a rogue hair protruding from the side of my nose. It shouldn't be there. I could shave it off but if I do that it will grow rapidly again; much better to pluck it. I find some tweezers. I am a man and therefore the pain of plucking is more than I can bear. But this is just one hair; surely even a man can endure a solitary pluck? With a determined snarl I grip the end of the hair with the tweezers and pull. I feel the sudden sharp pain run up and down my nose and also through my cheek on the inside. But I yank it anyway.

The agony is excruciating and I mist up the mirror with the breath of my screams. I blink through watering eyes at the tweezers. This seems to be an extraordinarily long hair! I tug again and again; and now hot tears have blinded my vision and my face is throbbing entire; the pain travels down my neck and branches out across my chest. I feel it spread deeper and deeper within me, reaching the very core of my being. But I continue pulling. I will extract this monstrous hair! And out it does come, but not before every inch of my frame has suffered.

I gasp and clutch the edge of the sink to prevent myself from falling in a swoon. Slowly my vision returns and clears. The tweezers have dropped out of my fingers. I realise now that the hair wasn't a hair but the end of a nerve that somehow poked it way out of my skin. It was connected to all my other nerves. I have accidentally extracted my entire nervous system, which coils around my feet like the spaghetti of torture. There is no way I am going to be able to put it all back in properly. Although in some ways I am calm; in others I am a bundle of nerves.

Wilson often has trouble falling asleep at night. This is partly because he suffers from insomnia and partly because he is artificial and doesn't need sleep. The two reasons might be the same. Only one method of getting to sleep seems to work for him, a variation on an old remedy recommended by grandmothers throughout Wales, namely the counting of sheep. Even clockwork men will doze off after counting sheep. But Wilson prefers to count clouds; and he doesn't want to do it one by one. That seems to him to be a very inefficient way of counting them. He has constructed a cloud grid to make the task easier and faster.

In this example, the grid consists of seven clouds across and seven clouds down. Seven multiplied by seven is forty-nine. This is a superior way of calculating the total than counting them individually. Wilson's real grid is rather bigger than this, of course. It is millions of clouds across, millions of clouds down. Wilson has an abacus mind. It takes lots of multiplication to send an abacus to sleep. The last time Wilson counted clouds in order to fall asleep the total was coincidentally exactly the same as the number of clouds that have ever rained on Wales.

There are no pockets on Welsh clothes. The inhabitants of this country hold their keys, wallets and other possessions in their hands. Welsh people have evolved large hands for this purpose. The trouble with pockets is that they rapidly fill with rain and the weight of the garments are increased substantially. We have already heard about Fiddly Buttons and Doodah Zips. When a man by the name of Rhodri Pouch ventured out in his brand new suit of clothes he was immobilized before he could reach the market that was his destination.

He was a Gothic feller just like Fiddly and Doodah and his clothes consisted of pockets sewn together, his trousers, shirt, jacket and hat made from overlapping pockets of various sizes. Some of these pockets were very deep, the sort that can be used to conceal a weasel. The rain poured into them and made his clothes heavier and heavier; and finally he was stopped dead in his tracks, too heavy to move, and he remained in that position as his pockets began overflowing and he became a human fountain until he eventually rotted away.

People who passed him threw coins into his pockets and made a wish, because that's what you do with fountains and also because it made their hands lighter.

It's not easy having to walk around clutching loose change all day, even if your hands happen to be extra big. These accumulated coins displaced the water but were even more effective at keeping him in place. When Rhodri had completely decayed, all that was left was a mound of wet pennies. Every wish was always for the sky to stop raining, but wishes don't come true, so it never did. If only Rhodri had taken shelter in his own largest pocket, he might have survived!

Or he might have died anyway from stress. The endless rain does create a lot of stress and stress is a major contributory factor to cancer. Rhodri Pouch was probably doomed from the very beginning of his journey to the market. He had hoped to buy tesques there; he had run out of tesques. I don't know why he didn't grow his own. It's easy to grotesques in the humps of any hunchback or gargoyle. Tesques thrive in the damp Welsh climate. No need to buy them.

Two charity workers happened to come past and they collected the pile of pennies for their charity. They were attempting to raise money for cancer. Often they would stand on pavements outside banks or shops and rattle their collecting tins while shouting, "Donations for cancer!" and people gave them coins for moral reasons and also to lighten their hands. "Thank you!" the charity workers always responded. They were persistent but polite. They were tireless fundraisers for cancer. Over the years they had raised tens of thousands of pounds, all in small change, and at the end of every session they would return along the gloomy streets to the place where they deposited the days' takings.

This was an ordinary house in a cul-de-sac. With the onset of twilight they would approach the front door and ring the bell. After a minute the door would be opened by a man dressed as a druid, one of the priests of the original pagan religion of Wales. The charity workers would go inside, pace down a corridor to the living room and pause on the threshold. This room was already knee deep in coins and they were beginning to spill into the corridor. The charity workers would empty their collecting tins into the room, increasing the total coinage by a small amount, and then turn to depart. "Good work, my children!" the druid would say, but he never smiled.

"Why are we doing this?" they sometimes asked him.

"You are collecting money for cancer. Cancer needs money."

"But why does cancer need it?"

A shrug. Druids are secretive. "To buy stuff with. One day there will be sufficient funds for cancer to purchase whatever cancer is planning to purchase. You must keep collecting. You are doing fine work. Cancer is pleased with you. . . ."

On one occasion, when the druid was distracted by a commotion in the garden that turned out to be a fight between two stray cats, the charity workers took the opportunity of going upstairs to see cancer for themselves. They found a vast tumour on a bed. It was bright red, festooned with strange protuberances, and it pulsated slowly. The mattress sagged under the weight. It had started life as a chicken heart. But it was growing rapidly and soon would fill the entire bedroom and then squeeze itself out onto the landing, growing at an accelerated rate until the house was no longer big enough to contain it. The bricks and mortar would fly apart and the heart would be loose, expanding in the rain, taking over the city, the country, the world.

The strange protuberances looked and acted like tentacles and there is an outside chance that the tumour was actually a manifestation of Cthulhu, the most notorious Lovecraftian monster. Lovecraft is one of those authors it is impossible simply to read and like or dislike. One is compelled to grapple with him thereafter, with his imagery, inferences, attitudes, with the morbid parts of ourselves he speaks to, even though we may reject that voice. His work is emotional, not intellectual. When we grapple with Lovecraft, we are grappling with ourselves; and this is a necessary thing, even if it feels more troubling than pleasant. His work embodies the flaws of his character but his neuroses resonate with ours. The pathological aspects of his vision are those of the human condition and it is pointless to protest that we are not made that way, that somehow we have risen above him entirely, that on no level at all do we share his fear of the new, his suspicion of the different, his hostility towards the outsider, his general timidity in the face of life. On some level, buried very deep perhaps, to a greater or lesser degree, we also possess those intolerances. He is a warning and an admonition as well as a fantasist. This is why he is still important.

I wonder if the hideous chicken heart was saving up for an airline ticket so it could escape Wales for a sunnier and drier region of the world? This is a common dream among the citizens of this country. The chicken heart had already collected enough money for a business class seat. Maybe it was holding out for a first class ticket. The three passenger classes of airline travel have always been an absurdity in the sense that first and business class don't arrive at the destination any more rapidly than economy class does. Yet they are much more expensive.

Mondaugen invented an aeroplane in which this absurdity was removed. The three classes were retained but now the passengers with the more costly tickets do arrive before the others. As soon as the plane takes off, the front part of the fuselage begins to extend itself. This is the section that contains the first class seats Then the middle section also separates itself and thus business class creates it own advantage over the economy class passengers. The plane keeps flying and the distance between the three sections continues to increase. The sections are joined together by powerful springs and hydraulic rods. The front part of the plane begins its descent and lands on the runway of the destination airport. It rolls to a stop. The first class passengers disembark. They pass through customs and leave the airport. The business class and economy class passengers are still airborne.

A few hours later, the business class section comes into land. The springs and hydraulic rods compress and contract. The middle of the fuselage rolls to a halt on the runway. These passengers also disembark. The economy class section is still in the air, its passengers being shaken by turbulence and staring glumly out of the tiny windows at ragged grey clouds. On short flights, for example from Wales to Spain, it is frequently the case that the front section of the plane has landed before the rear section has even taken off. The rain in Spain falls mainly on the plane. The entire craft resembles a metal rainbow with pots of passengers at both ends; one pot mixed with hope, the other pot, still grounded in Wales, suffused with gloom and despair and resignation.

This wasn't the first aeroplane Mondaugen ever invented. He once designed one in the shape of a boomerang that saves on fuel during the return journey. He also invented a terrifying cake that always came back. No matter how often you cut it, forked it, ate it, always it would still be there. An endlessly returning ghost cake. He called it the Boo Meringue. That's the kind of man he is. As for my fictional wife who was kidnapped by a Roman warrior: yes he did eat her. Tying up loose ends is important. And the Queen? Does she stand when the National Anthem is played; and if so, does this mean that self-praise gets a royal seal of approval? And if it does, how much smaller than a walrus is that seal?

I finally found the perfect tune for my oboe, the one I have travelled to so many different locations for. I found it in a most unexpected place, which perhaps is where I'd expected to find it. I knew deep down it wouldn't be any melody a human had composed.

A whale sang it to me one afternoon off the shore of a beach where I was paddling in the sea. I often paddle with an oboe, because I like to use the instrument to stir the yellow foam of the waves that lingers around my toes after the wave breaks and settles.

I thanked the whale for the gift and wondered how it happened that an animal of that kind should possess the secret of cloud music? The answer is that Whales and Wales are homonyms and homonyms are loyal to each other and try to be mutually supportive. The whale was The White Whale too, which made the experience nicer.

Needless to say I lost no time playing the special tune on my oboe and waiting to see what the clouds would do. But they did nothing. I was very disappointed. But then it occurred to me that maybe I was going about the process the wrong way. Maybe instead of blowing the magical tune down the oboe, I should be sucking instead?

I exhaled all my breath and when my lungs were empty I gently lifted the oboe to my lips, pointed the end at the sky and began sucking. For all I was worth and more, I sucked that melody. And it worked! I felt that the instrument was exerting a force on the heavens, pulling clumps of it down into the oboe. Then I understood that clouds must be vacuum cleaned out of the sky to get rid of them. There is no other way. I kept sucking harder and harder, always playing the melody.

My eyes were shut tight with the effort and I could only taste the parts of the sky that were being drawn down into the oboe, not see them. Now my lungs were full again, ready to burst. I had to stop to exhale, to let out the swollen air. I opened my eyes and the terrible thing I had done was in plain view. Stuffed in the end of the oboe was a ragged streamer of azure sky that flapped in the chilly wind like a poisoned tongue, broken, forlorn and dying. Instead of sucking the clouds from the dome above me, I had removed all the blue sky behind them.

So now I had condemned Wales to perpetual cloud cover. The forty-five days of clear skies a year, a paltry but welcome amount, had been minced by a misguided oboe. And the responsibility was mine! I was the villain of the piece. What an awful mistake! What an utter disaster! As I wept openly, collapsing to my knees like a prisoner hearing the sentence of death, the whale swam past again and said in my language, "That's revenge for the harpoons over all the centuries, buster!"

I like to think I'm a clever fellow. But I'm a sucker.

Sorry Wales! Sorry blue sky!

And it won't be long before the inhabitants of Wales take their anger out on me. Look, already here is Birdman Boyo flapping his homemade wings and circling high above. I gaze upwards at the oily speck that is his retributive form and I see that he is taking his trousers down. He squats in midair and strains; and even from this distance I can hear his grunts, but he is Welsh, his diet is stodgy; how can he move his bowels at will? The answer is that he can't and I am safe. . . .

Safe for the time being at least! It is clear there is no place for me left in Wales after this incident. I shall have to find a new home. Can I apply for asylum at the Embassy of Atlantis? It will surely be drier living on a drowned continent than in this country. I could marry a mermaid down there and then go into a bar and end up talking to a barmaid and complain that my marriage isn't working because my wife doesn't understand me. She only speaks Fish, whereas I am Welsh and speak Chips. Plus fluent Pies and Beer. And absolute Bollocks.

The circular bus full of reflections finally reached Egypt, dusty, battered, but intact and without losing any passengers. The border officials told the driver that the Pharoah was expecting them; that he was sitting on the lid of his sarcophagus in his pyramid, twiddling his bandages and waiting for them sedately. "He's a late dynasty Pharoah and they're much less formal about these matters," they added.

"What shall I do when I reach his pyramid?"

"Toot your horn," they said.

"Just toot it? Nothing else?" the driver persisted.

"Toot and come in."

"Ah yes I see! Tutankhamun . . ."

"No, no! Different Pharoah. The one you want is Psammetichus."

"I thought you said—"

"You know what thought did, don't you?"

"No, what did he do?"

"He thought he was, therefore I am, but you aren't included. Now stop holding up the traffic and move on!"

The driver put the bus into gear and drove away.

They passed through Egypt.

An ancient realm of colours and shadows, sounds

and metaphors and descriptive passages through which the notes of reed flutes seem to play plaintively, while dark-eyed girls beneath crescent moons dance in a style that might be construed as exotic and sultry, and desert winds sing softly tonight, and the palm trees waver, and crocodiles snap at the incense that drifts in serpentine threads across this entire paragraph, and jackals laugh at jokes told around the local oasis. . . .

The driver parks next to a modestly sized pyramid. "This is the address."

The reflections in the mirrors squirm.

"Are we there yet?"

The driver nods. "We've arrived," he says.

"Ooh, we don't like it."

"How can you be sure? You haven't got off yet."

"We want to go home!"

"Not before the Queen obtains the secret. Please stop making problems and follow me into the structure."

"What does the silly old Queen want the lost secret of mummification for so badly anyway? Surely it would be much easier to go to Veracity to drink the elixir of youth, if longevity is really her thing? Why doesn't she do that instead of sending us here?"

"No point trying to understand a monarch's mind. It's not your place to question her commands, but merely to obey. The Queen orders you to locate the secret and return with it."

Grumbling and sparkling, the reflections climb down onto the ground and follow the driver around the base of the pyramid to a small door. The driver rings the bell. Deep within the stone building there is a tinkling so faint that it sounds like a distant star weeping into a crystal glass. This is followed by the shuffle of bandaged feet along a corridor. It takes fifteen minutes before the door is opened.

A fully wrapped mummy, a little frayed around the edges, stands and nods at them from the doorway. "Sorry it took so long for me to answer, my legs are completely desiccated; I can only move them very slowly. It isn't far to my sarcophagus. Come inside please. You are my guests and I am happy to receive you. She's a great pal of mine, the Queen, and rulers always have to stick together, just like, oh I don't know, any comparison that is valid! Tonsils and throats!"

"Humpty and Dumpty," suggests the driver.

"That's a good one. Gins and tonics! Mustard and cress! Donkeys and carrots! Bears and popes! Messengers and shootings! Buggers and rashes! Similes and metaphors! Gimps and jerks! Custard and rhubarb! Flippancy and mirages! Boners and dancing!"

"Boners and dancing?" queries the driver.

"Yes, yes! Have you never danced close with a woman? The boner is an epiphenomenon of the experience. No, you haven't? You don't dance because you are Welsh? Oh, I see, you dance like a chess piece. So there is no close contact. Well, that's to be expected, I guess. But talking about chess reminds me. The chess pieces stored in my pyramid keep muttering they've got nothing to do. The counters for backgammon are making the same complaint. . . . Bored games, huh?"

"I have never yet danced close with a woman."

"Surely you have hugged one?"

"I have hugged many!"

"The boner principle is exactly the same with a hug as with a dance. A hug means something different to women than it does to men. To women it is a comforting gesture of communication, of friendship, trust, warmth, compassion and empathy. It expresses unconditional and non-acquisitive affection. But to men it is a narrowing of the distance between the boner and its target destination. I am just telling it the way it is! Don't shoot the messenger! Not unless you're the Pope!"

"Messengers and shootings . . ."

"Indeed so! One of the most common pairings."

"Rain and Wales," says the driver.

"Ha ha! That's the spirit. Well, no actually the spirit is the whisky in a barrel that preserves a plethora of monkeys in my sarcophagus room, but the less said about that, the better."

"You're an extraordinary man," decides the driver.

"Yes, but my reign was weak. 526 BC to 525 BC. That's only one year and I lasted just six months of it. The Persians invaded and defeated me soundly at the Battle of Pelusium and I had to flee to Memphis where I went into hiding but was captured and then executed. It was a really bad time that I prefer not to think too much about. But anyway, just down this passage and to the right. Here we are!"

The driver and reflections enter the sarcophagus room and stand about rather aimlessly. It is crowded in there now, but the Pharaoh doesn't seem to notice the discomfort of his guests. He sits back down on the coffin lid and swings his legs and rubs his hands.

"So how can I help you?"

"The Queen wants to know the lost secret."

"What of? There are many."

"Mummification."

"Ah, the lost secret of mummification!"

"Yes. Do you have it?"

"I certainly do and it's a very easy one to share. In fact I think you are going to be disappointed that you've come all this way just to be told one word that describes a concept that you could have worked out for yourself if you'd made the attempt. And you really didn't need to bring these other people with you. There's nothing heavy to carry or anything like that. It's just one word that any ear can hold."

"What is the word? What is the lost secret?"

"The lost secret of mummification, I am happy to tell you, is nothing more nor less than daddyfication."

The driver and reflections blink at each other.

"Daddyfication?"

"Indeed," confirms the Pharoah.

"Just that on its own?"

"Perform the mummification as normal, then add daddyfication, that's all there is to it. This technique is called the 'family way' and guarantees a successful continuation of the person who's being treated down through the generations. So now you know!"

The driver turns on his heel, the reflections stumble after him, they all climb back on the bus and the vehicle drives away. The Pharoah shrugs at this rudeness. It's all the same to him.

The return journey is mostly uneventful for the bus and its passengers. The driver retraces his route through Lebanon, Turkey, and all the nations they have already passed through, and no drama or tragedy takes place at all until the final stages of the last day.

Unable to repress her excitement that she is about to learn the secret of mummification at last, the Queen jumps off her throne and runs, crown wobbling, to meet the bus. It has been raining and the road is wet. A fine mist floats in the air. Visibility is bad.

She jumps out in front of the approaching vehicle and waves for it to stop. The driver slams on the brakes but it is too late. The bus skids and connects with the impetuous monarch!

The Queen is thrown high and as she tumbles in midair, the costume she is wearing splits open. The driver and his passengers are astonished to see that inside the Queen is another being. It's the Dutch tourist Van der Graaf. But now he strikes the road and his costume splits asunder too. He also has another being inside him. But who? Birdman Boyo! Who despite his injury, flaps his wings and takes off.

But while he is ascending, his costume also splits and reveals another being inside, Primella Limpet, who descends gently due to her billowing petticoats. But of course she splits too and reveals Boxhound Rummage, who has enjoyed his time inside her. Yet he also splits apart and now we see that Fiddly Buttons is back! But only for a moment because he splits to disgorge Doodah Zips, who also splits.

Inside him is Cloudier Sheepier; inside her is Rudyard Kipling; inside him is Dr Moreau; inside him is Haon Why; inside him is Dylan Thomas; inside him is Nazrat del Sepa; inside him is Vera the alchemist; inside her is Meeky Chunky, which must have been a really tight fit; inside him are the other incidental characters who have appeared in this work so far; and thus it continues, this series of surprises.

The entity now standing in the middle of the road is Mondaugen. But he also splits to reveal Wilson the Clockwork Man. And finally Wilson splits with a brassy sound like a trumpet chewed by a hippo. The collision with the bus ruptured all these costumes one inside the other. The seams of all of them tore open. And inside Wilson is Richard Brautigan, his hat askew and his shirt a little rumpled, and his expression somewhat ironic. I often store characters inside each other.

The story is over now, if a story is what it was.

Let's have the ending!

My favourite ending to any work of fiction comes from another Brautigan book. Choosing the ultimate 'best' ending from the thousands of books I have read in my lifetime is perhaps too difficult a task, but the ending of *A Confederate General from Big Sur* saves me the trouble of doing that because it is an ending about endings, a meta-ending, and the only thing it brings to an end is the worry about constructing a brilliant ending. It presents a solution to a problem faced by every author through the ages, namely providing the right ending to a text, and it does this by making other endings the purpose of its ending.

> Then there are more and more endings: the sixth, the 53rd, the 131st, the 9,435th ending, endings going faster and faster, more and more endings, faster and faster until this book is having 186,000 endings per second.

I won't be able to match the excellence of that ending.
But here is mine:

> Rain, rain, go away! Come again another day. On second thoughts, don't ever come back, you little damp bastard. . . .

We often hear about 'spontaneous human combustion' but almost never about 'well planned and carefully organized (with budgetary stringencies not exceeded) human combustion'.

In Wales we never hear about either kind. It is simply too wet here for people to burst into unexplained flames.

How is the word 'either' pronounced? I usually say 'either'; some people say 'either'. I guess either is correct.

We often hear about the Attack of the fifty foot Woman but centipedes have twice that many feet and nobody makes a fuss. We often hear about the Incredible Shrinking Man but I feel sorrier for the Untalented Shrinking Man. In Wales all men shrink in the rain.

Dylan Thomas was originally one mile high. The rains gradually shrank him in the wash but he forgot he was no longer a giant and kept drinking the amount of beer a giant would, even though he was now only as tall as a short man. I don't know how to prevent people shrinking in the rain but I know plenty of other things, so I have decided to compile a brief list of my indispensable wisdom. Here it is:

- Trumpets in the pantry are unusual.
- When the stairs creak too loudly go upstairs on the outside instead.
- The face in the teaspoon is generally yours.
- If you fancy a bit on the side then walk not forwards or backwards.
- Better to grunt loudly when eating a pickle than to ride a bicycle dressed as a panda.
- Never employ a tyrannosaur as a short hand typist.
- Wearing a corset outside a dress is like wearing a skull outside a hat.
- Existence precedes essence, especially vanilla essence.

The text is coming to an end. It is still a WIP, a work in progress, but not for much longer. There is a knock on my door. I am not expecting visitors at this hour. I wonder who it can be?

The park behind the university is flooded today. This is partly because the rhododendrons were labelled a 'nuisance' and cut down in the summer. If they were still standing their roots would have drunk some of the rain and kept it inside the tree. Rhododendrons aren't a nuisance! Income tax is a nuisance; bubonic plague is a nuisance; drunken men shouting at night in the streets are a nuisance. Rhododendrons are beautiful and right. Leave them alone and leave all trees alone and pitch-fork all Tree Surgeons over cliffs into the sea instead! That's what I say.

I open the door and find myself confronting both Wilson and Mondaugen. They enter without waiting to be invited. They have inscrutable faces but they seem in a rush. "The end of the prose is approaching, we must move fast, there's no time to lose!" they declare. Then Mondaugen picks me up and inserts my head into the keyhole in Wilson's back. I neglected to say that my head is shaped like a key. That's one advantage of not describing characters early on in the text. You can make them look any way you like later on. My head's shaped like a key.

"Does he need winding up so badly?" I splutter.

"I am using you to wind him the wrong way," explains Mondaugen as he rotates my head savagely in the slot.

"But why?" I screech.

"To sabotage his failsafe mechanism."

"He'll go into meltdown."

"Yes! and burn his way through the Earth's crust and continue down, down, down, through the core and back out the other side. We will cling to his limbs as he does so. Hold tight! We are getting out of the country, this saturated sponge called Wales. We will start again, the three of us, in a place where it doesn't rain every single fucking day of our lives, where we have a chance to be unsplashed."

"Can this really work?"

"It can, oh it can! Freedom and dryness!"

"Keep winding him then!"

"I will, I will. I won't stop until . . . Oh!"

"What has happened?"

"The key snapped. . . . Your head. . . . I'm sorry."

> "When it is misty, in the evenings, and I am out walking by myself, it seems to me that the rain is falling through my heart and causing it to crumble into ruins."
>
> (Gustave Flaubert)

OK rain, you've made your point. . . . You are sky water. You fall out of big dark fluffy sky sheep called clouds. You give the plants a drink. You make overlapping concentric circles on puddles and ponds and lakes like a college lecturer explaining Venn diagrams. You trickle down the back of my neck like the opposite of erotic fingertips. . . . I understand you and your game. You can stop now.

There is nothing more to teach me.

Are you listening, rain! Why are you ignoring me?

Wilson heaves a sigh of weary relief. "That's it for another year, the flock of clouds finally dipped one by one. How many were there in total?" and he turns his stiff neck to look at me. I shrug my shoulders. "I don't know, I wasn't keeping count," I answer him.

He is annoyed by this admission and shakes his crook as if preparing to discharge its stored electric current into me. "But you were supposed to be numbering them as they went in! Maybe some wandered off and got lost in the minds of those who read them."

I don't see why that should be my task. I only came to visit him on his hillside cloud farm, not to work for him as well. I tell him this and he rubs his brass chin thoughtfully, shakes his head and says slowly, "Don't you realise who and what you actually are?"

Although in Wales one tends to stand with hunched shoulders because of the rain, I stand erect and proud. "I am a man, a real man," I reply. I am pleased with myself for making this declaration, but Wilson suddenly laughs uproariously and cries, "Oh that's a good one! I must tell that to Mondaugen. What a hoot! What a jape!"

"I don't see what's so amusing," I answer curtly.

"Whatever gave you the idea you are a man? You were

designed and constructed by Mondaugen, just the same as me. We are both artificial. I can't believe you haven't worked it out."

This news devastates me but I know it's the truth.

"I'm a clockwork man too?"

"Not a man," he corrects me, and then in a more kindly tone he adds with a small smile, "I'm a cloud farmer. Cloud farming is very similar to sheep farming. Sheep farmers use sheepdogs to keep their flocks in order and cloud farmers use clouddogs. That's what you are, my friend. You're a synthetic clouddog and I control you by whistling. Your job is to round up the clouds, protect them from predators, number and count them when they are dipped. But sheepdogs get old and must be retired; and I suspect that the same thing is true for clouddogs."

"I am fifty years old. That is still quite young!" I cry.

"Not for a clouddog, I'm afraid."

"Have I always been a clouddog or was I once something else. Was I never a flesh and blood human male?"

"Just a clouddog dreaming he is a man; and not a man dreaming he is a clouddog. I am just telling it the way it is. Don't shoot the messenger! Not unless you are the Pope, that is."

"I beg your pardon?"

"Don't shoot me unless you are the Pope."

"You really mean that?"

"Of course I do. Only he is permitted to shoot messengers thanks to a precedent set by a fable long ago."

And now my chance has come! I reach with wet but eager fingers for the zipper that runs from the top of my head all the way down my body. I unzip myself and reveal my true form! I am the Pope and my musket is loaded and even though Wilson is made from metal I doubt he'll enjoy the impact of a stone bullet on his hide.

Wilson's reflexes are rapid. He swings his crook and points it at me. Stalemate! This is a Vatican standoff. The clouds roam about unattended but there's nothing we can do about that. We are stuck in this situation. I think we'll still be here like this, facing each other, until the end of time. Which means it is time to say adios!

FINIS

A PARTIAL LIST OF SNUGGLY BOOKS

LÉON BLOY *The Tarantulas' Parlor and Other Unkind Tales*

FÉLICIEN CHAMPSAUR *The Latin Orgy*

BRENDAN CONNELL *Clark*

QUENTIN S. CRISP *Blue on Blue*

QUENTIN S. CRISP *September*

LADY DILKE *The Outcast Spirit and Other Stories*

BERIT ELLINGSEN *Vessel and Solsvart*

JUSTIN ISIS *Divorce Procedures for the Hairdressers of a Metallic and Inconstant Goddess*

VICTOR JOLY *The Unknown Collaborator and Other Legendary Tales*

JEAN LORRAIN *Nightmares of an Ether-Drinker*

JEAN LORRAIN *The Soul-Drinker and Other Decadent Fantasies*

JEAN LORRAIN *Masks in the Tapestry*

CATULLE MENDÈS *Bluebirds*

KRISTINE ONG MUSLIM *Butterfly Dream*

YARROW PAISLEY *Mendicant City*

DAVID RIX *A Suite in Four Windows*

FREDERICK ROLFE *An Ossuary of the North Lagoon and Other Stories*

JASON ROLFE *An Archive of Human Nonsense*

TOADHOUSE *Gone Fishing with Samy Rosenstock*

TOADHOUSE *Living and Dying in a Mind Field*

CPSIA information can be obtained
at www.ICGtesting.com
Printed in the USA
BVOW03s1149260617
487853BV00001B/11/P